# CREATURES OF THE NIGHT

Blade could see the Vampire's glassy eyes widening in consternation. He raised the M-16 to his right shoulder,sighted, and fired. His initial rounds smacked into the lead Vampire's head, catapulting the ghoul backwards.

Sergeant Havoc, Boone, and Thunder took their cue from the Warrior. Each cut loose with skilled precision.

Caught in the open in a withering spray of automatic gunfire, the Vampires were decimated. Six dropped in half as many seconds, their bodies riddled with holes. Two foolishly tried to reach the bus and were cut to ribbons. Only one was left alive; he wheeled and attempted to flee.

Also in the BLADE series:

# BLADE

## #3 VAMPIRE STRIKE

— DAVID ROBBINS —

LEISURE BOOKS ⬛ NEW YORK CITY

Dedicated to . . .
Judy & Joshua & Shane.
And to Bram Stoker,
who started the ball rolling,
and Jeff Rice and Anne Rice
for superbly upholding the tradition.

A LEISURE BOOK

August 1989

Published by

Dorchester Publishing Co., Inc.
276 Fifth Avenue
New York, NY 10001

Printed in the United States of America.

# PRELUDE

But first on earth, as Vampyre sent,
Thy corpse shall from its tomb be rent;
Then ghastly haunt thy native place,
And suck the blood of all thy race;
There from thy daughter, sister, wife,
At midnight drain the stream of life;
Yet loathe the banquet, which perforce
Must feed thy livid living corse.
Thy victims, ere they yet expire,
Shall know the demon for their sire;
As cursing thee, thou cursing them,
Thy flowers are withered on the stem.

Lord Byron
*The Giaour*
*1813*

# PROLOGUE

The Vampires were aboard.

Ethan Hogue felt his skin tingle as he gazed at the forest bordering the asphalt road. On both sides the dense walls of murky vegetation reared toward the inky sky and the canopy of stars. He heard a rustling noise to his left and raised the lantern in his right hand overhead to increase the radius of its illumination.

"Did you hear something, Ethan?" his sister asked nervously.

"No," Ethan lied. "No, Greta, I didn't."

Greta glanced at the lantern, then at the trees to the left. She knew he was lying, but she refrained from reprimanding him. He was trying to quell her anxiety, and she loved him the more for his concern. "How far are we from Aguanga?"

Ethan stared down the roadway. "A mile. Maybe less."

"We should hurry," Greta urged. She brushed at her blonde bangs.

"Fine by me," Ethan said with a forced nonchalance.

They increased their pace.

Ethan placed his left hand on the Astra Model 357, snug in its brown leather holster on his left hip. The feel of the checkered walnut stocks reassured him and served to calm his jittery nerves. Perhaps he was wrong, he told himself. Perhaps the rustling he'd been hearing for the past five minutes was nothing more than the breeze stirring the nearby foliage. Or perhaps the cause was a harmless nocturnal animal. He shook his head to clear his mind of a vague premonition of doom. What a dope! He was letting his worry get the better of him! A few lousy noises and he was ready to crap his pants! The Vampires had not been reported in the vicinity of Aguanga in over a year.

So why was he getting all bent out of shape?

Ethan grinned at his idiocy, his brown eyes twinkling.

"What's so funny?" Greta asked.

"Look at us," Ethan said. "We're acting like six-year-olds instead of mature adults!"

"A person can never be too careful at night," Greta commented.

"Traveling at night isn't as dangerous as it once was," Ethan remarked. "The Raiders haven't operated in this area for more than a decade, according to Dad, and the Army wiped out most of the mutants. The worst we can bump into is a hungry rabbit."

"I hope you're right," Greta said.

"I know I'm right," Ethan assured her.

"I guess we shouldn't have stayed so late at Aunt Harriet's," Greta mentioned.

"Why not?" Ethan responded. "Aunt Harriet and Uncle Brice are fun to be around. We owe them a visit every now and then."

"I still can't understand the reason they live so far out of town," Greta said.

"What's to understand?" Ethan queried. "They like their privacy."

Greta frowned. "Maybe so. But I know I would never live two miles from the nearest village or city. I like the security of having others close at hand."

"The trouble with you, sis," Ethan observed, "is that you have a postwar mentality."

"What's that supposed to mean?" Greta demanded.

"World War Three took place over a century ago," Ethan noted. "Yet you, and a lot of other people, act like the war ended recently. You seem to think that California is sitll crawling with muties and Raiders, when it isn't. Oh, there are some, but they're confined mainly to the mountains and the uninhabited stretches. The area around Aguanga is relatively safe. There's no reason in the world a person can't live outside of town.''

"You're forgetting the Vampires," Greta said.

"I'm not forgetting them," Ethan stated. "But a Vampire hasn't been seen around here in a long time."

"They'll show up again," Greta declared.

"You don't know it for sure," Ethan disagreed. "They may never come back."

"They'll be back," Greta insisted. "They know there are hundreds of women living in or near Aguanga."

"How would they know that?" Ethan inquired.

"They have their ways," Greta said.

Ethan snickered. "You've been listening to the old-timers. They believe the Vampires are endowed with supernatural powers."

"Don't you?" Greta questioned.

"Hell, no," Ethan said. "There must be a logical explanation for the Vampires and their activities."

"Like what?" Greta queried.

"If I knew the answer," Ethan said, "I'd be famous. I'd lead an expedition to the Dead Zone and wipe them out."

"No one has ever gone into the San Diego Dead Zone and lived to tell about it," Greta remarked. "No one in their right mind would enter a Dead Zone."

"The Vampires live in the Dead Zone," Ethan said. "And the only way to destroy them is to find their base and exterminate them."

"Maybe the Vampires live in the Dead Zone," Greta mentioned. "Maybe they don't. All we have to go on is rumor."

"Where else could they live?" Ethan questioned. "They must have a base somewhere."

There was a sharp retort to their right, the distinct snapping of a branch.

Both halted.

"What was that?" Greta asked apprehensively, her green eyes wide.

Ethan scanned the forest, his left hand tightening on his revolver. He debated whether to extinguish the lantern. Without the light, Greta and he would be harder to spot. Both were wearing dark clothing; he wore brown pants and a black shirt, while his sister was wearing green slacks and a cinnamon-colored blouse. But whatever was lurking in the woods might possess better night vision. If he turned out the lantern, they would have the advantage. He decided to leave the lantern on.

"Let's keep going," Greta advised.

Brother and sister hastened onward. The night seemed exceptionally still and silent. Not so much as a cricket chirped.

Once Ethan thought he detected a glimmer of white to his right. He surveyed the vegetation, but he could see nothing out of the ordinary.

"Look!" Greta exclaimed happily after several minutes.

A cluster of lights were visible ahead.

"Aguanga!" Ethan declared, intensely relieved. He ran his left hand through his brown hair.

"I can't wait to get home," Greta said.

They pressed forward until the first residence was discernible, outlined against the backdrop of the ebony heavens by a bright porch light. The interior lights were all out.

"McCallister's," Ethan commented.

"I hear they got a new dog," Greta said.

"Yeah," Ethan confirmed. "I saw it yesterday. A big, mean mongrel. If anyone comes within ten feet of their fence, the mutt barks like crazy." He paused. "I also saw Bob yesterday. He says he's thinking of asking you to the dance."

"What?" Greta responded in surprise. "I didn't know Bob likes me."

"He's seventeen, you know," Ethan said.

"So? I'm twenty, and I don't date boys," Greta stated stiffly.

"I wouldn't call Bob a boy," Ethan said. "And since when did you become so fussy about the guys you date? You keep this up, and you'll be an old maid."

"You wouldn't understand," Greta said.

"What's to understand? My sis is stuck up," Ethan declared.

"I am not!" Greta responded.

Ethan stared at the McCallister house as they stepped onto

the sidewalk next to the wooden fence. The front porch was ten yards away.

"That's odd," Greta commented.

"What is?" Ethan inquired.

"Where's their dog?" Greta asked. "I thought you said it barks at anyone who comes near their fence."

"Maybe they took it inside for the night," Ethan suggested. "Bob was taking a liking to the mutt."

Greta scrutinized the McCallister home, wondering if there was any significance to the dog's absence. She took another step, then abruptly stopped, her eyes narrowing.

Ethan halted. "What's the matter?"

"Their front door is open," Greta said.

Ethan gazed at the house. The front door was indeed open a hands-breadth. "So?"

"Why would they leave their front door open?" Greta queried.

"Give me a break!" Ethan replied. "They're probably letting some fresh air in. What's the big deal?"

"Go check," Greta said.

"What?" Ethan responded. "You're nuts. I'm not about to make a fool of myself."

Greta looked at her brother with a pleading expression. "Please, Ethan. For me?"

Ethan sighed. "What am I supposed to say when one of them comes to the door?"

"You'll think of something," Greta assured him. "Please do it. I have a bad feeling about this."

"Over a stupid door being open?" Ethan said testily.

"Please," Greta insisted.

Ethan gave in. He never could refuse his sister. "Okay. I'll go check. I just hope their dog doesn't attack me." He extended his right arm. "Here. Take the lantern."

Greta took the lantern and lifted it above her head.

"I'm going to look like a dope," Ethan mumbled as he gripped the top of the gate, a slatted affair painted white like the rest of the picket fence.

"Be careful," Greta said.

"Nothing will happen," Ethan asserted flatly, then pushed

on the waist-high gate. Normally the gate would swing inward on well-oiled hinges, but not this time.

The thing wouldn't budge.

Perplexed, Ethan tried to open the gate again with the same result. It moved a fraction, then stopped. He knew the McCallisters had not bothered to install a lock on the gate.

So why wouldn't it move?

Ethan leaned over the top of the gate and spied the vague form sprawled at its base. He froze, his eyes registering the distinctive black and white markings he'd seen on the McCallister's new dog. The mongrel was lying flat on its side.

"What is it?" Greta inquired.

Ethan leaned over the gate, striving to recall the dog's name. Homer. Bob had told him the mutt was named Homer. "Homer! Remember me!"

Homer remained motionless.

"What is it?" Greta repeated, taking a step toward her brother.

"I don't know," Ethan said, reaching down to pat the dog. Was the mutt asleep? His right hand patted the dog's head and started to stroke its neck. A sticky substance caked his fingers. He straightened, horrified, insight dawning. Of *course* the dog wasn't asleep!

The mongrel was dead!

"Ethan?" Greta said, touching his right shoulder.

Ethan raised his right hand into the lantern light. He gaped at the crimson coating, dazed. Fear flooded over him as he realized the truth; his earlier premonition had been correct. He'd managed to convince himself everything was okay, but now he knew better. He should have heeded his presentiment.

The Vampires were in Aguanga!

Greta spotted the blood on his hand and gasped.

"We're heading home," Ethan declared. He wiped the blood off on his pants leg.

"The McCallisters . . ." Greta said, staring at the house.

"Forget them," Ethan stated, drawing his revolver. "We need to worry about Mom and Dad."

"You don't think something has happened to them?" Greta questioned in alarm.

"Let's find out," Ethan said grimly.

They raced to the north through an unusually quiet town. Except for the streetlights and a few porch lights, Aguanga was dark and eerie.

Ethan gazed at an unlit house to the right. Not everyone would be asleep at this time of night. There should be homes with their inside lights on. But there weren't any.

They reached an intersection and took a left.

"Look!" Greta exclaimed. "They have their lights on!"

Frame houses lined both sides of the street, four on each side, and all of the homes were amply lit except for the first residence on the left. But even as they watched, the second house on the left went totally dark.

"Mom and Dad!" Ethan cried, racing along the sidewalk toward the last home on the left. His home.

Greta sprinted alongside her brother, the lantern bobbing and swaying in her hand.

They were abreast of the third home when all the inner lights flicked out.

"Damn!" Ethan snapped in mounting frustration. His black boots pounded on the sidewalk.

"Please!" Greta said in despair. "Please!"

They came to the edge of the Hogue property, an acre of land with the house situated 20 yards from the street, and angled across the front lawn.

Ethan took the lead, dashing for the front porch. He was 25 feet from the cement steps leading to the porch before he perceived the front door was wide open. "No!" he shouted, cocking the Astra on the run.

From within the Hogue residence arose a terrified screech.

"Mom!" Ethan cried. He reached the steps and darted onto the porch. Ignoring his own safety, he plunged into the house.

Every light was simultaneously turned off.

Ethan stopped in the center of the pitch-black living room. Someone must have killed the current to the house! But how? He squinted, waiting for his eyes to adjust, and listened. "Dad? Mom?"

There was no answer.

Ethan cautiously moved toward the rear of the house, toward

the kitchen. He leveled the Astra, his finger caressing the trigger.

A sibilant titter sounded upstairs.

"Dad? Mom?" Ethan called, turning and heading for the stairs. He knew the house like the back of his hand, and he could navigate in the dark with ease. Skirting the couch and a rocking chair, he arrived at the base of the stairway and paused.

Someone tittered again.

His gun arm steady, he advanced up the stairs. He was three steps from the top when he halted. In his haste and anxiety over his parents, he'd completely forgotten about his sister! Where was she? Waiting outside? He couldn't see the glow of the lantern anywhere below.

What if something had happened to her!

"Greta?" Ethan yelled.

A foul stench suddenly assailed his nostrils.

Ethan faced the top of the stairs, his breath catching in his throat at the sight of the pale, scarecrow-like figure perched above him wearing only a black loincloth. Glassy eyes glared at him.

A Vampire!

Ethan squeezed the trigger as the Vampire swung its right arm. Excruciating agony rocked his jaw and his head was lashed backwards. His ears ringing from the deafening boom of the Astra, stunned by the Vampire's blow, he tottered on the brink of the step.

The Vampire snarled and struck a second time, a hard fist to the midriff.

Ethan lost his balance and tumbled down the stairs. He landed on his back at the bottom, bruised and battered and stunned. Shaking his head to clear his sluggish mind, he rose onto his elbows.

With a hiss like an enraged cat the Vampire began to descend the stairway.

Frantic, overcome by abject fright, Ethan heaved to his feet and spun. He ran out the front door to the yard.

"Ethan! Help me!" Greta screeched from off to the left.

Ethan peered into the night, catching sight of four white shapes loping to the south. One of them appeared to be carrying a burden draped over its left shoulder.

"Ethan! Help!"

The burden was Greta!

Ethan raced in pursuit of the four Vampires and his sister. The creatures seemed to flow over the ground, avoiding obstacles with consummate ease.

"Help!" Greta wailed.

Gritting his teeth in determination, Ethan poured on the speed. He was one of the fastest young men in Aguanga, but his speed was inconsequential compared to the unearthly swiftness of the Vampires.

"Ethan!" Greta cried in despair, her voice growing fainter.

Ethan refused to acknowledge defeat. He kept after them, covering five hundred yards, then a mile.

The Vampires were barely visible.

For over two miles Ethan chased the vile creatures. Twice he tripped and almost fell. Once he banged his shins on a small boulder. He crossed a field, a stretch of forest, and another field.

Where were they?

The Vampires had vanished in a thick stand of trees.

An acute pain was developing in Ethan's right side. His breathing was ragged, and his legs were ready to buckle at any moment. He reached the stand of trees and halted, leaning on a trunk for support.

He'd lost them!

And lost his sister!

Ethan sagged to his knees, misery engulfing him. No one had ever been rescued from the clutches of the Vampires. He would never see his sister again! Tears welled in his eyes, but he suppressed the impulse to cry. Instead he rose unsteadily and shuffled toward Aguanga. His parents were still in the town, and although the possibility of their being alive was remote, he could not simply abandon his folks. The Vampires specialized in abducting young women; a middle-aged couple would not appeal to them in the least except as victims of their renowned blood lust.

A stiff wind from the west stirred his brown hair.

He needed a plan. Ascertaining whether his parents were alive was the first step. Should he go from house to house afterward searching for survivors of the raid? Or should he locate a telephone? Phones were a rare luxury in Aguanga. The Upshaws owned one, and hopefully they had already used it to call for help. Unfortunately the phone lines in rural areas were beset by problems and service was deplorable. World War Three had totally disrupted all utilities and forms of mass communication, and while some semblance of order had been restored, conditions were a far cry from their former efficient estate.

A twig cracked behind him.

Ethan turned, his reflexes sluggish. He caught only a glimpse of a pale figure holding an object in its hands, and then that object crashed into his forehead and the world abruptly tilted on its axis. Cimmerian darkness engulfed him, and with a groan Ethan pitched into oblivion.

# CHAPTER ONE

The pair of thundering jets swooped out of the northwest, dropping to treetop level in seconds and roaring toward Highway 79. They streaked over a large clearing adjacent to the highway and banked in a tight loop, their speed rapidly decreasing. Both jets slowed to a complete stop above the clearing and hovered for 30 seconds, then sank to the grass accompanied by a muted whine.

A small door located just under the center portion of the canopy on the jet nearest the road opened and a green rope ladder unfurled to the ground. The first occupant appeared, a veritable giant of a man squeezed through the doorway and clambered down the ladder. He turned and stared at the two jeeps parked alongside the highway. The giant stood seven feet in height, and his awesome physique was powerfully muscled. His eyes were gray, his hair dark with a comma hanging over his brows. A black leather vest and green fatigue pants served to clothe his massive form. A Bowie knife was in a leather sheath on each hip. In his left hand was a Commando Arms Carbine. A camouflage backpack rested between his shoulder blades. He moved several feet from the jet, then raised his right fist overhead and pumped it three times.

Both jets disgorged other figures.

The second man down was a lean six-footer attired in buckskins. His shoulder-length hair was brown, as were his keen eyes. A matched pair of Hombre revolvers were strapped around his lean waist. He carried an M-16, and like the giant he toted a backpack.

Next came a full-blooded Indian wearing a fringed buckskin shirt, pants, and moccasins. Black hair fell past his broad shoulders. His brown eyes scanned the nearby vegetation as he adjusted his backpack with his left hand while cradling an M-16 in his right arm.

From the second jet came three more. A slim woman climbed to the ground. She wore fatigues, combat boots, and a backpack. An M-16 was held in her left hand. Fine brown hair draped almost to the small of her back. Her face was exceptionally attractive, hightlighted by her alert brown eyes, her high, prominent cheekbones, and thin lips.

Next down was a man who radiated an air of supreme confidence. He stood six feet tall and weighed close to 200 pounds, and every square inch was solid muscle. He was wearing a brown T-shirt, fatigue pants, and black combat boots. His backpack was snug against his back. An M-16 was slung over his right shoulder, and like the Indian and the woman he was armed with a pair of Colt Stainless Steel Officers Model 45's in holsters on each hip. His blue eyes gazed at the jeeps.

The last to appear was decidedly different from the others. Unlike the rest, the only clothing he wore was a black loincloth. Unlike the others, his sole weapon in evidence was an M-16. And unlike his companions, his five-foot-eight frame was covered with a coat of short, light brown fur from head to toe. His face resembled that of a bear; he had a receding brow,deep, dark eyes, circular ears, concave cheeks, and a pointed chin. His elongated nostrils flared as he sniffed the air, and his lips curled upwards to display a mouthful of tapered teeth. Both his upper arms and shoulders were especially dense and rippling with layers of muscle.

The giant waved his right arm toward the jeeps, and the others keyed on his signal and formed a single file behind him as he advanced to the side of Highway 79. The morning sun was warm, the air humid.

A portly, balding man dressed in beige pants and a brown shirt was seated at the wheel of the closest jeep. He smiled as he slid out and extended his right hand. "Hello. I'm Cyrus Upshaw. You must be Blade."

The giant nodded as he shook Upshaw's hand. "Yes. Thank you for meeting us."

Upshaw was impressed by the giant's steely grip. He released Blade's hand and motioned at the jeep. "Thank you for coming. Why don't we get in and I'll explain everything on the way to Aguanga?"

"Good," Blade said. He glanced over his right shoulder at his unit. "Grizzly and Athena with me. Boone, Thunder, and Havoc in the other jeep."

The party promptly divided, each member taking a seat in the appropriate vehicle.

Upshaw reclaimed his position at the wheel.

Blade sat down on the passenger side. "Ready when you are," he commented.

Upshaw glanced at the jets. "What about them?"

"They'll be flying back to Los Angeles in a few minutes," Blade replied.

"I've never seen jets like those," Upshaw mentioned. "What are they?"

"VTOLs," Blade answered. "They can attain supersonic speeds, yet they also possess vertical-takeoff-and-landing capabilities."

"Like a helicopter," Upshaw observed.

"Sort of," Blade said. "They transport us wherever our assignments take us."

Upshaw started the jeep. "I've read about the Freedom Force in the papers, but I never thought I'd meet all of you in person."

"The Force goes where it's needed," Blade remarked. "If trouble develops anywhere in the Freedom Federation, we're sent to deal with the situation."

Upshaw pulled out, heading the jeep to the south. He gazed

in the rearview mirror to insure the second jeep was following him. "The Federation leaders had the right idea when they formed the Force," he said. "Taking one volunteer from each Federation faction and creating a special, elite fighting team was brilliant."

"And necessary," Blade stated. "It's been one hundred and five years since World War Three. The seven factions composing the Freedom Federation face constant threats to the Federation's existence. We needed a combat-ready strike force to deal with the menaces that continually crop up."

Upshaw looked over his left shoulder at the bear-man seated in back of the giant. "I forget. Which Federation faction is he from?"

"I can talk, you know," the bear man declared in a raspy tone. "The name is Grizzly, and I'm from the Civilized Zone."

Upshaw made a coughing noise. "Sorry. I didn't mean to upset you."

"I'll bet," Grizzly cracked dryly.

"You're a mutant," Upshaw noted. "Or more correctly, a hybrid."

"No fooling!" Grizzly retorted. "What was your first clue?"

"You know what I mean," Upshaw said defensively. "We don't see many mutants like you in California. Oh, there are a lot of the wild kind, the mutations produced by the enormous levels of radiation and all the chemical toxins unleashed on the environment during World War Three. We see more than our share of three-headed animals and other deformities. But we don't see many like you."

"That's because I'm the result of genetic engineering," Grizzly said. "Genetically developed hybrids aren't as numerous. We're unique," he added proudly.

Upshaw negotiated a curve in the highway. "It's hard to believe how much the country has changed since World War Three. The government of the U.S. collapsed, and now we have a lot of groups scattered all over the landscape. California was fortunate. We were one of the few states to retain our administrative identity after the war."

"True," Blade spoke up. He reflected on the current state of affairs resulting in his present mission. Seven factions had banded together into a protective alliance dubbed the Freedom Federation. The Free State of California, as it was now called, had been the last member admitted to the Federation. The governor of California, as a token of good will and commitment, had graciously offered to base the Federation's new tactical unit, the Force, in Los Angeles, and to utilize California's VTOLs as the primary means of transport. And here he was, the leader of the Freedom Force, leading his people into action once again. He hadn't expected to be sent on a mission so close to LA. Aguanga was approximately 80 miles from the metropolis.

"I know about the Civilized Zone," Upshaw was saying. "How the remnants of the U.S. government withdrew to Denver during the war and reorganized a new government in the Midwest. I also know about the other Freedom factions." He glanced into the rearview mirror. "Which one is the young lady from?"

"Mr. Upshaw, meet Athena Morris," Blade introduced her. "She's our newest addition to the Force, and she hails from California."

"Really?" Upshaw said in surprise.

Athena leaned forward. "Is there something wrong with having a woman on the Force?"

"No," Upshaw stated hastily. "Of course not. But it wasn't mentioned in the papers."

"I just joined, officially, about three hours ago," Athena disclosed.

"What did you do before you joined the Force?" Upshaw asked.

"I was a journalist for the *Times*," Athena replied.

"Say!" Upshaw exclaimed. "Aren't you the one who's been writing all those features on the Force? I seem to remember your byline."

Athena beamed. "You do, huh? Yep, that's me."

"Why would a journalist want to join the Force?" Upshaw inquired. "You're putting your life on the line every day."

"It's simple," Athena said, lowering her voice conspiratorially. "I'm as crazy as the rest of these turkeys!"

"Speak for yourself, wench," Grizzly chimed in.

Upshaw glanced at Blade. "You have quite a crew, don't you?"

"You don't know the half of it," Blade said.

"Refresh my memory," Upshaw prompted. "Where are the others from?"

"The Indian you saw, Thunder, is a Flathead from Montana," Blade detailed. "The gunman with the revolvers is Boone, and he's from the Dakota Territory. And the soldier, Sergeant Havoc, is the best noncom in the California military. He has black belts in karate and judo and a brown in aikido."

Upshaw's forehead creased. "There are two members from California in the Force? I thought it was supposed to be one from each Federation faction?"

"We've been forced to make some adjustments," Blade said. "We've already lost two men. One was from the Clan, and the second was sent by the Moles, both of which are based in Minnesota."

"Isn't the group you're from based in Minnesota too?" Upshaw queried.

"Yes," Blade confirmed. "The Family lives in northern Minnesota, in a compound designated the Home."

Upshaw grinned. "Quaint names."

"The man who founded our survivalist compound believed in certain basic values," Blade explained. "He incorporated those values when he formed his survivalist retreat."

"I've read a lot about you," Upshaw went on. "They say you were the head of the Warriors, the guardians of the Home."

"I still am the top Warrior," Blade mentioned. "I've been juggling both responsibilities."

"You head the Warriors and the Force?" Upshaw said. "You must be one tough son of a gun."

"Him? He's a cream puff," Grizzly interjected.

"Now that we've satisfied your curiosity," Blade said to Upshaw, "why don't you fill me in on what happened here last night?"

"Gladly," Upshaw said. "Aguanga was hit by the Vampires."

"The Vampires?" Blade repeated quizzically.

"You've never heard of them?" Upshaw inquired.

"Just in passing," Blade said. "When General Gallagher proposed this assignment, he told me a town had been raided by them. But he didn't go into detail. I assumed he was referring to a band of Raiders."

"There wasn't enough time for Gallagher to explain everything," Athena stated in the general's defense. Gallagher had been instrumental in helping her to get onto the Force despite Blade's initial objections, and she felt she owed the general a debt.

"True," Blade conceded. "We were sent out on short notice."

"Besides," Athena stated, "I can fill you in on the Vampires. I know as much about them as anyone. I've seen scores of stories on them."

"Be my guest," Blade said.

"The Vampires first appeared about seventy years ago," Athena elaborated. "They've raided small communities and towns every year or so since then. They always attack at night. They've completely wiped out a few settlements—"

"What is the purpose behind their raids?" Blade asked, interrupting. "Are they after food? Valuables? What?"

"Women, primarily," Athena said. "They've abducted hundreds of wolmen, and a few dozen men, in the seven decades they've been raiding southern California."

"Why do they take so many prisoners?" Blade questioned.

"No one knows for sure," Athena responded. "There are a lot of rumors. Some people say the Vampires suck the blood of their captives."

"Are you serious?" Blade asked.

"According to the rumors, the Vampires feast on the blood of their victims," Athena stated. "We both know how unreliable rumors can be."

"I suppose I shouldn't be shocked," Blade remarked. "After all the cannibals, mutants, scavengers, and other degenerates I've encountered, blood-sucking deviates are nothing unusual."

"Are you familiar with the legend of the Vampires?" Athena inquired.

"No," Blade admitted.

"You told me once that your Family has hundreds of

thousands of books preserved in a concrete building," Athena commented. "Don't any of those books deal with vampires?"

Blade pondered for a moment. "I can recall a book from my schooling days. A friend of mine named Geronimo did a book report on it. The novel was by a writer called Stoker, I believe. The story concerned a vampire, a Count-somebody-or-other."

Athena grinned. "Count Dracula. He was the title character in a book called *Dracula* published in 1897."

"You seem to know a lot about the subject," Blade noted.

"I'm a journalist, remember?" Athena responded. "Any journalist worthy of the name performs lengthy background research on a story to be covered. I had to write up a few of the Vampire stories for the *Times*, and naturally I conducted a study of the vampire legend in general," Athena explained. "Legends concerning vampires have been around for as long as the human race has been in existence. Traditionally speaking, vampires were regarded as inhuman creatures, either corpses or spirits who arose from the dead to feast on the blood of the living. Scores of books and films featured the vampire in one form or another before the war."

"But vampires aren't real," Blade said.

"So far as we know," Athena stated. "But the legends have persisted for ages. So when the raids began seventy years ago— always at night, and always by creatures seemingly endowed with supernatural powers—it's understandable why the creatures were called Vampires."

"What else do we know about them?" Blade probed.

"Not much, I'm afraid," Athena said. "They usually kill all witnesses to their raids."

"Where do they come from?" Blade asked.

Athena shrugged. "No one knows. The Army has attempted to find their lair without success."

Upshaw cleared his throat. "Some people believe the Vampires come from a Dead Zone."

"What's the Dead Zone?" Grizzly inquired.

"Not *the* Dead Zone," Athena corrected the mutant. "*A* Dead Zone. Dead Zones are areas that sustained a direct nuclear hit during the war."

"My Family refers to them as Hot Spots," Blade said.

"Whatever," Athena declared. "San Diego suffered a direct hit, and Aguanga is only sixty miles away."

"Aguanga was fortunate," Upshaw interjected. "Aguanga was just outside the blast radius, and the prevailing winds blew the radiation to the southeast, sparing the town."

"Why do some people believe the Vampires come from the San Diego Dead Zone?" Blade questioned.

"Because the Army has tracked them to the edge of the Dead Zone twice," Athena answered. "Each time the Vampires had raided a town and taken a lot of captives. Each time the Army used dogs to follow the trail. And each time the trail led into the Dead Zone."

"Did the Army go in after them?" Blade asked.

"Once," Athena replied. "The first time."

"And what happened?" Blade asked.

"The platoon never returned," Athena disclosed.

Blade lapsed into a reflective silence. Was it possible, he speculated, that General Gallagher had deliberately refrained from revealing all the pertinent information pertaining to the Vampires because the general had been afraid the mission would have been turned down? As the head of the Force, Blade exercised veto power over every proposed assignment. Perhaps, knowing the Force had just returned from a deadly strike in Oregon, the general had intentionally withheld the full scope of intelligence available on the Vampires for fear Blade would decide the unit wasn't up to another sustained conflict so soon after Oregon.

Perhaps.

But he lacked proof.

So, for the time being at least, he would extend Gallagher the benefit of the doubt.

"What are you thinking about?" Athena queried.

"Nothing," Blade told her.

"Look!" Upshaw declared, staring at a cluster of buildings ahead. "There's Aguanga."

# CHAPTER TWO

Aguanga was a typical community, arranged with a network of side streets encircling a small central business district consisting of a few old-fashioned stores.

Cyrus Upshaw drove through the town until he reached an intersection with a STOP sign. He pressed on the brakes briefly, then took a right. "The southwest section of Aguanga was hit the hardest," he elaborated. "I suspect the Vampires approached town through the Cleveland National Forest. They must have bypassed the Mission Indian Reservation because no one spotted them until they were in Aguanga."

"What tactics did they employ?" Blade inquired.

"They're a crafty bunch, I'll grant them that," Upshaw stated. "They waited until it was late, ten o'clock or so, before they came in. There were dozens of them, and they'd hit an entire street at one shot. Their usual technique involved killing the power to a residence, then entering. All women between the ages of sixteen and thirty, or thereabouts, were taken prisoner. Very few men were taken. Most of the men were killed."

"How many homes were attacked?" Athena asked.

"Forty-four," Upshaw answered. "Aguanga has grown a lot since the war. Our population is slightly over two thousand." He paused and frowned. "The raid could have been much worse than it was."

"How many casualties were there?" Blade questioned.

Upshaw's cheeks seemed to sag. "Seventy-three were slain. Thirty-two women are missing and five men. Surprisingly, they spared the youngest children." He stared at a house on the left, the fourth in a row. "There's the Hogue home. There's a young man here worth seeing. His mother and father were killed last night, and his older sister is one of those missing."

"Why should we see him?" Blade queried.

"He's one of the few who actually got a glimpse of the Vampires," Upshaw replied. "Even tried to shoot one. The fiends nearly split his skull wide open." He executed a tight U-turn and parked alongside the curb.

Blade stared at the homes lining the street. "Did you have guards posted around the town?"

"No," Upshaw said. "What good would it do? The Vampires possess acute senses. They'd spot our guards long before the guards saw them. The guards would have been killed needlessly. They wouldn't have helped last night, and they wouldn't have helped a year ago."

"What happened a year ago?" Blade inquired.

"Three women disappeared," Upshaw responded. "We never did find them despite an extended search. No one saw them being abducted, but everyone believes the Vampires were responsible."

"The Vampires seldom strike the same town twice in a row," Athena commented. "Aguanga is an exception. Usually the Vampires range all over southern California. Predicting their attacks has been impossible."

Upshaw turned the key and the jeep's engine sputtered and stopped. He climbed out. "Do you want to talk to the Hogue boy?"

"How old is he?" Blade asked.

"Nineteen," Upshaw replied.

"Is it all right to disturb him?" Blade questioned.

"The doctor said a short visit was permissible," Upshaw said.

"Okay. But we won't stay long," Blade stated. He emerged from the jeep, then bent over to gaze at Grizzly and Athena. "Wait here."

"I'd like to come," Athena said.

"The fewer who go in, the better," Blade responded. "It sounds like our witness is very seriously injured. We don't want to strain him more than absolutely necessary."

"Do you want us to twiddle our thumbs while we're waiting?" Grizzly quipped.

"You can sharpen your claws," Blade suggested and straightened. He walked to the second jeep, now parked to the rear of the first.

Sergeant Havoc was seated on the passenger side across from the driver. "Orders, sir?" Havoc asked out the window.

"Stay put," Blade directed.

"Yes, sir."

Cyrus Upshaw started toward the Hogue home. "If you'll come with me . . ." he said to the giant.

"Ethan Hogue is a fine young man," Upshaw commented. "I knew his father and mother well. I'll miss them."

Blade followed Upshaw onto the porch. "Tell me," he said. "How were the seventy-three casualties killed? Was the blood drained from their bodies?"

"No," Upshaw replied. "Most of those killed were husbands and the older sons or brothers of the kidnapped women. And women over thirty or so were also killed. Ethan's mother, for instance, was forty-nine. In every case their death was violent, brutal. Either their necks were snapped or their throats were torn apart." He shuddered at the memory.

"Let's go in," Blade advised.

Upshaw knocked on the wooden door and waited.

Within seconds a plump, elderly woman in a gray dress opened the door. "Mayor Upshaw! What a surprise."

"Harriet," Upshaw said, "I'd like you to meet Blade, the leader of the special team the governor sent to take care of the Vampires. Blade, this is Harriet Tofani, Ethan's aunt."

"Hello," Blade stated.

"I'm pleased to meet you," Harriet mentioned. "It's about damn time the Vampires were eliminated!"

"We'll do our best," Blade assured her.

"Harriet, we need to see Ethan," Upshaw informed her. "Doc Cook gave his permission."

Harriet stepped to one side. "Come on in. Ethan is upstairs, resting in bed. Doc Cook says he won't be on his feet again for at least two weeks." Her mouth curled downward. "The poor boy! And to think of sweet Greta in the hands of those monsters!"

Upshaw moved toward the stairway. "We'll only be a few minutes."

"Would you like some tea?" Harriet asked Blade.

"No, thanks," the Warrior responded.

"How about some cookies? Or cake? I have a chocolate cake fresh out of the oven."

"Thank you. But not now," Blade told her. He stayed on the mayor's heels as Upshaw went up the stairs and took a left, proceeding to a bedroom at the end of the hall. The door was open.

Blade towered a foot and a half over the mayor. He could see into the bedroom as they walked down the hallway, and he spied the Hogue youth on a bed against the far wall. Ethan Hogue's head was swaddled in white bandages and his eyes were closed.

Upshaw tapped lightly on the door jamb.

Ethan opened his eyes and swiveled his head in the direction of the doorway, grimacing in discomfort. "Mayor Upshaw," he said thickly, then licked his lips.

"Doc Cook said we could talk to you for a few minutes," Upshaw stated. "Are you feeling up to it?"

Ethan's eyes shifted to the giant.

"This is Blade," Upshaw explained. "He's the head of the Force."

Ethan's eyes brightened. "I've read about you," he said weakly.

"Are you up to talking?" Upshaw reiterated.

"Sure," Ethan replied.

The mayor and the Warrior stepped over to the bed.

"How are you feeling?" Upshaw asked.

"A little better," Ethan answered. "The doctor gave me

something for the pain. Now all I have is a dull ache.'' He tried
to grin. ''And twenty-one stitches, of course.''

''Ethan,'' Blade said, ''I'll make this as short as possible.
I understand you actually saw the Vampires. Is that right?''

''Yes,'' Ethan confirmed.

''Can you describe them?'' Blade questioned him.

''It was dark,'' Ethan began. ''I couldn't see them clearly.
I stood within a few feet of one of them, but I was scared to
death at the time. All I remember is very white skin. They were
real thin too. And they didn't wear much clothing.'' He paused.
''Oh. They can run like deer. I've never seen anyone run as
fast as they can.''

''Did you note any facial features?'' Blade asked the youth.

''No,'' Ethan said. ''Sorry.''

''Don't be sorry,'' Blade told him. ''You were under great
stress.''

''Is there anything else you can tell us?'' Upshaw interjected.
''Anything that may be important?''

Ethan reflected for a moment. ''Yeah. The four I went after,
the ones who took Grace, were heading to the south.''

''That's good,'' Blade said. ''It narrows down the area we'll
need to search to find their trail.''

''There's not much else I can help you with,'' Ethan remarked
forlornly.

''Did you see any weapons?'' Blade thought to ask.

''No,'' Ethan responded. ''None of the Vampires carried guns
or knives or anything. But one of them did hit me with something.''

''Your Uncle Brice found a big, bloody rock near where he
discovered you,'' Upshaw disclosed. ''The Vampire hit you
with the rock.''

''I don't have any further questions,'' Blade commented. He
turned to leave.

''Blade . . .'' Ethan said softly.

Blade glanced at the young man.

''They took my sister!'' Ethan exclaimed, tears filling his
eyes. ''Please don't let them kill her! Bring her home safe and
sound!''

Upshaw placed his right hand on Ethan's shoulder. ''Calm

down, son. Blade and his people will do everything in their power to save Greta and the others. You get some sleep now.''

Ethan mustered a feeble smile. ''Okay.'' He closed his eyes and instantly dozed off.

Blade descended to the living room, Upshaw behind him.

Harriet Tofani was sitting in a blue easy chair, knitting. She went to rise.

''Don't get up,'' Blade said. ''We'll let ourselves out.''

''Are you sure you won't have some tea and cake?'' Harriet asked.

''We have work to do,'' Blade stated. He smiled and exited the home.

''Can we lend you any assistance?'' Upshaw inquired as they returned to the jeeps.

''Thanks,'' Blade stated, ''but from here on out, it's up to us.'' He halted on the sidewalk between the vehicles. ''Fall in,'' he barked.

The Force members promptly climbed from the jeeps and formed a single line on the sidewalk as the Warrior backed onto the grass. They stood at attention awaiting their instructions. Athena was on the right, then Grizzly, Boone, Thunder, and Sergeant Havoc.

Blade clasped his hands behind his broad back. ''Thirty-two women and five men were abducted from this town last night by Vampires. Our objective is twofold: to save those who were kidnapped and to exterminate the Vampires.''

''Blade,'' Boone interrupted. ''What in the world are Vampires?''

''I don't know,'' Blade admitted. ''They could be humans, mutants, or hybrids. Whatever they are, they've been raiding southern California for seventy years. The Force is going to put a permanent end to their depredations.''

''Sir,'' Sergeant Havoc declared. ''Do we have an estimate of enemy strength?''

''Enemy strength is unknown,'' Blade answered. ''A conservative guess would be several dozen, minimum. But there could be hundreds.''

Grizzly grinned. ''My kind of fight.''

''Our first step is to find their trail,'' Blade directed. ''Grizzly,

I want Thunder and you to conduct a sweep pattern. Start in the back yard of this house. I doubt the Vampires could completely cover their tracks, not with thirty-seven captives in tow. Get moving.''

Thunder and Grizzly jogged off.

Mayor Upshaw, standing near the second jeep, shook his head. ''The Vampires never leave tracks. Our best hunters couldn't find their trail.''

''The Army has tracked them twice,'' Blade noted.

''But they used dogs,'' Upshaw mentioned.

''Thunder is an outstanding tracker,'' Blade said. ''If they leave so much as a smudge on the ground, he'll find it. And as for Grizzly, his sense of smell is better than a bloodhound's. They'll pick up the trail.''

''What about us?'' Athena asked.

''We wait,'' Blade replied. He stared at the lanky gunfighter. ''Boone, get General Gallagher on the horn.''

Boone knelt, placed his M-16 on the sidewalk, and removed his backpack. He unfastened the upper flap, revealing a compact military radio.

''I understand you're from the Dakota Territory,'' Upshaw commented while watching the gunman fire up the unit.

''From the Cavalry,'' Boone said, referring to the Federation faction in control of the Dakota Territory.

''What do you think of California?'' Upshaw asked.

''Let me put it this way,'' Boone said, adjusting a black headset with an adjustable boom mike over his ears. ''I can't wait until my hitch is over and I can return to Dakota.''

''Force members serve for a year, don't they?'' Upshaw queried.

''Don't remind me,'' Boone stated. He flicked a toggle and began talking into the mike. ''Bravo-Lima-Alfa-Delta-Echo to Big Bad Wolf. Repeat. Bravo-Lima-Alfa-Delta-Echo to Big Bad Wolf. Do you copy? Over.''

Mayor Upshaw's face betrayed his bewilderment at the military jargon.

A small, square speaker in the upper right corner of the radio suddenly crackled with static. ''This is Big Bad Wolf speaking,'' a gruff voice declared.

"One moment for Sir Galahad," Boone said, removing the headset and extending it to Blade.

Feeling slightly self-conscious at having to use the general's code words, Blade took the headset and aligned the band over his head. "Silent mode," he said to Boone.

The Cavalryman flicked another toggle and the speaker on the unit ceased crackling.

Blade could hear the static in his headphones. He spoke into the boom mike. "Sir Galahad here."

"Do you have something to report?" General Gallagher inquired.

"We expect to start in pursuit shortly," Blade replied.

There were several seconds of silence, as if the general expected additional information. "Is that all?" he demanded.

"Why wasn't I provided with a complete dossier on the Vampires?" Blade inquired bluntly. He could envision the bulldog of a general turning crimson with anger.

"What do you mean?" Gallagher hedged.

"Don't play games with me," Blade said sternly. "You know what I'm referring to."

"Speed was of the essence," General Gallagher maintained. "There wasn't time for a complete briefing before your departure."

"Perhaps," Blade said. "In any event, we're going to have a discussion about this after I return to the Force HQ."

"Whatever you want," Gallagher commented. "I'll be here until the mission is accomplished. If you need anything, just say the word."

"I need more honesty," Blade stated. "Sir Galahad, over and out." He stripped off the headset and tossed it to Boone.

"Do you mind my asking what was that all about?" Mayor Upshaw queried.

"General Gallagher and I don't always see eye to eye," Blade explained.

"Did he rush you down here?" Upshaw asked.

"You can say that," Blade responded.

"Maybe he was justified," Upshaw remarked. "You wouldn't want the trail to become cold."

"Speaking of the trail," Sergeant Havoc interjected and

pointed to the right.

Blade turned. Grizzly and Thunder were running toward him. ''Find anything?'' he asked them.

Grizzly smirked and nodded. ''Let's go kick some Vampire butt!''

# CHAPTER THREE

"If it wasn't for the captives," Thunder remarked as he knelt in the middle of a field seven miles from Aguanga, "tracking these Vampires would be next to impossible. They tread lightly and rarely leave even a partial print."

"At least we won't lose them," Blade said. He glanced at Grizzly, standing to his left. "What about the scent?"

"Human, I'd say," Grizzly opined. "Not very pungent, though. Sometimes you humans stink to high heaven, but these suckers don't. They must bathe regularly."

"And we don't?" Athena rejoined.

"I have my doubts," Grizzly replied, then snickered.

"Let's keep going," Blade directed. "We still have plenty of daylight left."

Grizzly and Thunder resumed their tracking, working in tandem.

Blade waited until the mutant and the Flathead were 20 yards ahead before motioning for the others to follow. Athena was behind him, Boone next, and Sergeant Havoc brought up the rear.

"The Vampires have changed direction," Athena remarked.

"I noticed," Blade said. Initially the Vampires' trail had proceeded due south from Aguanga, but six miles from the town the trail angled to the southwest.

"The San Diego Dead Zone is southwest of here," Athena noted.

"Which means the Vampires may be heading for their home base," Blade deduced. "And once we locate it, we can dispose of them."

"Mind if we talk?" Athena inquired.

Blade glanced over his right shoulder. "About what?"

"You."

"Why are you so curious about me?" Blade asked, facing front and watching Grizzly and Thunder enter a stand of trees.

"I'm curious about everyone on the Force," Athena answered. "I need copy for the stories I file on our escapades. The more background information I obtain, the more human interest angles I uncover, the more my readers will like my articles. And we want the public to perceive the Force in a favorable light. You know as well as I that there are those who think the Force is an unnecessary waste of taxpayer dollars. General Gallagher, for one. He opposed the Force when the unit was formed, and he hasn't changed his opinion."

"Gallagher opposed the Force on political grounds," Blade reminded her. "He believes California should not have joined the Freedom Federation. He's an isolationist. He thinks the state is better off by itself."

"Whatever his reasons," Athena said, "he's not our biggest booster."

"He must like you," Blade observed. "He tried repeatedly to persuade me to allow you to join."

Athena elected to change the subject. "How are your wife and son? Have Jenny and Gabe adjusted to life in Los Angeles?"

"Not yet," Blade said, and sighed. "Jenny misses Minnesota. She wants to live at the Home, not in California."

"What will you do if she goes back?" Athena asked.

"I don't know," Blade replied. "I'll cross that bridge when I come to it."

"Maybe you should take her on a vacation," Athena proposed. "We could all use some R and R."

"I think you're right," Blade agreed. "After this mission is over, everyone will receive a two-week leave." He walked into the trees.

"Terrific!" Athena said happily. "Now all I have to do is survive the mission."

"I know I could use two weeks off," Boone interjected. "I'd like to visit some friends in Dakota."

"Are those friends female?" Athena asked impishly.

Boone shrugged. "One or two."

"I thought so," Athena snickered. "Any plans for marriage in the near future?"

"My personal affairs are none of your business," Boone informed her.

Athena looked back at the Cavalryman. "Touchy, aren't we?"

"I'm not a Californian," Boone responded.

"Meaning what?" Athena pressed him.

"Yeah," Sergeant Havoc joined in. "What's wrong with Californians?"

"You want the truth?" Boone asked him.

"What else?" Havoc rejoined.

"Californians, for the most part, have lost their edge," Boone assserted.

"What edge?" Athena asked, delighted the gunman was conversing freely. Usually, Boone was laconic, bordering on silent. Of all the Force members, only Thunder was less talkative. She knew very little concerning the backgrounds of both men, and she was determined to learn more, to uncover their motivations and beliefs.

"I never realized it until recently," Boone said. "The people living before the war must have been soft, flabby, and lazy."

"Why do you say that?" Athena probed.

"Because the people living before the war and Californians today have a lot in common," Boone stated. "Many of them, particularly those in the big cities like Los Angeles, can't hunt or fish worth beans. They'd starve if they ever had to fend for themselves. All their necessities—their food, their clothing, their water, and whatnot—are provided for them. They don't know how to be self-reliant. They let others do their thinking for them." He paused. "If the people living before the war were the same, then it's no wonder their civilization crumbled."

"Are you saying all Californians are the same?" Sergeant Havoc queried.

"Nope," Boone responded. "There are exceptions, like yourself. You can take care of yourself better than most men I know, but you're a professional soldier. You've been in the military all your life."

"And I suppose life is different in the Dakota Territory?" Athena questioned.

"As different as night and day," Boone told her. "Folks in the Dakota Territory know how to live off the land. Living on the frontier hardens people, men and women. We wouldn't fall apart if the grocery trucks stopped delivering food because we can grow our own."

"So you think the people living in the Dakota Territory are superior to those in California?" Athena said, goading him.

"I never said that," Boone answered, correcting her. "I simply said the folks in Dakota are more self-sufficient. We haven't lost our edge. We haven't lost touch with ourselves."

"Interesting," Athena commented.

"There's something I'd like to know," Sergeant Havoc said.

"What is it?" Boone asked.

"If I remember my history, wasn't there a North and South Dakota at one time?" Havoc questioned.

"There was," Boone verified. "But the two merged after the war. Both states became known as the Dakota Territory. The Cavalry controls the southern half, but we're having problems in the north."

Blade, listening to the conversation while keeping his eyes trained on Grizzly and Thunder as the Force weaved through the trees, abruptly halted. He gazed at the Cavalryman. "What kind of problems?"

"Some of our patrols have been ambushed," Boone detailed. "And a few farms and ranches were destroyed."

"By whom?" Blade inquired.

"We don't know," Boone said. "Kilrane is planning to mount a major campaign to find out next month."

Blade's gray eyes narrowed. Kilrane was the leader of the

Cavalry and a friend. "Why wasn't the Federation Council apprised of the situation?"

"We can handle it ourselves," Boone stated.

"After our leave is over, maybe we can fly to the Dakota Territory and show the Cavalry how to kick butt, as Grizzly would say," Athena suggested.

Sergeant Havoc laughed.

"I don't like the idea of Kilrane keeping secrets from the other Federation leaders," Blade said. "Why did we go to all the trouble to form the Federation if we're not going to rely upon one another when trouble arises?"

Boone didn't respond.

Blade looked to the southwest. Grizzly and Thunder were nowhere in sight. Annoyed, he marched after them. The others followed.

Athena surveyed the trees. "Anyone have an ax?"

"Why do we need an ax?" Blade asked.

"To chop down some of these trees. We could carve a couple of dozen dandy wooden stakes."

"Wooden stakes?" Boone repeated quizzically.

"According to legend, the only way of killing a vampire and insuring it stays dead is by driving a wooden stake through its heart." Athena explained. "Legend also has it that you can kill a vampire by chopping off its head, sprinkling it with Holy Water, or exposing it to sunlight. But there is evidence to suggest those means do not dispatch the vampire forever. The best method is the stake."

Boone glanced at the trees. "What did these vampires supposedly look like?"

"They were invariably reported as pale and thin," Athena disclosed. "They possessed long fangs and were incredibly strong."

Blade suddenly recalled the words of Ethan Hogue: "All I remember is very white skin. They were real thin too."

"Vampires were reputed to have the ability to transform themselves into bats in some cultures," Athena was saying. "Their breath was the pits." She paused. "Oh. And they could run like the wind. One report of a vampire in Las Vegas in the 1970's claimed the creature attained speeds of fifty to sixty miles an hour.''

Blade remembered Ethan's statement: "They can run like a deer. I've never seen anyone run as fast as they can." Was it possible, *really* possible, vampires were more than mere myth?

Sergeant Havoc snorted derisively. "It's all bunk! There are no such things as vampires!''

"Don't let them hear you say that," Athena teased. "They may try to suck your blood tonight."

"I'd like to see them try," Havoc stated. "I bet a vampire can't suck much blood with a 45 shoved up its nose.''

Boone chuckled.

"I don't think you two have anything to worry about," Athena said. "The Vampires we're after seem to prefer the fairer sex."

"Don't worry, Athena," Sergeant Havoc stated. "We wouldn't let a Vampire get its grubby hands on you."

"How sweet! I didn't know you cared," Athena quipped.

"We wouldn't want to give the Vampire blood poisoning," Havoc elaborated.

The soldier and the Cavalryman enjoyed a hearty laugh.

Blade was pleased to note their newfound sense of amiability. On the first mission, and again during the Reptilian affair, intense friction between them had reduced their effectiveness and threatened the existence of the Force. It was nice to see them getting along for a change. The others had even accepted Grizzly as one of their own, although initially they had resented his presence in the unit. He hoped they would continue to grow in their mutual friendship. If not, they—

A burst of automatic gunfire suddenly erupted from up ahead.

# CHAPTER FOUR

**B**lade galvanized into action at the first sound. He raced in the direction of the shooting, skirting trees and crashing through the underbrush. Irritated at himself for losing sight of his point men, anxious for their safety, he discarded all caution.

A tremendous growl rent the air.

Had Grizzly and Thunder encountered the Vampires?

Blade heard a guttural roar arise 20 feet in front of him. He sprinted around a large tree, covered 15 feet in a mad dash, and plowed through a shoulder-high bush.

There they were!

Thunder was down, prone on the ground, a trickle of blood seeping from his left temple, his M-16 beside him.

Eight feet from the Flathead was the cause of his condition: a mutant. Like so many of the mutations affecting the animal kingdom, this one stemmed from the embryonic deformity produced by the contaminated environment. Radioactive and chemical toxins had leeched in to the soil and entered the food cycle. A healthy, pregnant animal would drink tainted water or consume poisoned plants and thereby drastically alter the formation and development of the embryo it was carrying.

This one, once, would have been a black bear.

Now it was a raving, insatiable demon.

On all fours it stood four feet at the shoulders and was seven feet in length. A coat of ragged, patchy black hair covered its seven hundred pounds of sinews and muscles. In contrast to a normal bear, the mutant's head was outsized, twice the typical length. Most of the hair on its head was missing, exposing dry, cracked, sickly skin. Saliva dripped from its gaping maw, its huge teeth glistening with drool. Between the shoulder blades was an extraordinary hump, a trait characteristic of the grizzly bear, not the black.

Even as Blade watched, the mutant reared up on its hind legs and shuffled toward Thunder.

Standing between the mutant and the Flathead was Grizzly. He had cast his M-16 aside and was crouching with his arms at his sides. His hands suddenly went rigid, his fingers fully extended, and five-inch claws shot from his fingers and thumbs.

Blade had witnessed Grizzly employing those retractable claws before. The claws were housed in the upper portion of Grizzly's hands, above the knuckles. When Grizzly straightened his hands and locked them in place, the claws automatically popped out, sliding down sheaths just under the skin and issuing from underneath small flaps of flesh located behind each fingernail. Once his hands were locked and the claws extended, Grizzly could not use his fingers for anything other than ripping and slashing. Which suited him just fine.

Grizzly abruptly sprang, pouncing on the bear's chest and burying the claws on his left hand in the mutant's chest. He blocked a ponderous swing of the bear's arm with his right, then raked the bear across the eyes.

The mutated bear snarled and tried to embrace its tormentor in a lethal hug.

Grizzly dropped to the grass and ducked to the right. He darted around his foe and vaulted onto the mutant's back.

Blade, fascinated by the furious battle, held his fire for fear of accidentally striking Grizzly. He was dimly aware that the others had arrived and were likewise transfixed.

Grizzly tore into the mutant's neck with a vengeance, tearing and stabbing.

The mutant, growling in rage, lumbered toward a tree. It pivoted and attempted to pin Grizzly against the trunk.

But Grizzly was too quick. He released his grip and jumped to the left, landing and launching himself again in a fluid motion. His claws speared into the mutated bear's eyes, all the way to the fingertips.

The bear stiffened and tottered forward. Its mouth opened and closed a few times.

Grizzly, clinging to the bear's oversized head, raised his right arm overhead, then buried his claws in the bear's left ear.

With a gurgling grunt the bear toppled over.

Grizzly was already dropping to one side. He landed lightly on his feet and straightened. His claws were caked with blood and gore.

The mutated bear was on its stomach, crimson spurting from its ruptured eye and its left ear. It convulsed and wheezed, nearly dead.

Thunder groaned and opened his eyes. He began to rise.

Blade moved to the Flathead's side and used his left arm to assist Thunder in standing.

Athena walked over to Grizzly. "Are you okay?"

"I'm fine," Grizzly replied. "This bear was a wimp. I didn't even work up a sweat."

"What about you?" Blade asked Thunder. The Flathead was sagging against him.

Thunder reached up and gingerly touched his left temple. He ran his fingers over a two-inch cut below the hairline. "I feel groggy," he said. "But I don't believe my injury is serious."

Blade looked at Grizzly. "What happened?"

The hybrid nodded at the bear. "The sucker jumped us. Thunder was in the lead and saw it coming. He got off a few rounds, but the thing never stopped. It clipped him on the head."

"Why didn't you use your M-16?" Blade demanded. "Why did you rely on your claws?"

"Thunder's rounds didn't have any effect," Grizzly replied, then smirked. "Besides, I like the personal touch."

"Overconfidence can lead to disaster," Blade observed. "You shouldn't take unnecessary risks."

Grizzly grinned. "Can I quote you in my biography?"

"Grizzly was magnificent," Athena stated in his behalf. "He saved Thunder's life."

Grizzy beamed.

Sergeant Havoc stepped over to the mutated monstrosity. "I don't see what all the fuss is about. It's just a dinky bear."

"Oh, yeah?" Grizzly said, his eyes narrowing. "I'd like to see you take on a mutant using only your hands."

"I could have wasted this bear with one hand," Sergeant Havoc declared.

"Bet me!" Grizzly rejoined.

"I could," Sergeant Havoc stated.

Grizzly glanced at Blade. "And you think *I'm* over-confident?"

"You don't believe me?" Sergeant Havoc queried in mock surprise.

"Do I look like I was born yesterday?" Grizzly retorted.

"One hand is all it would take," Sergeant Havoc insisted. He reached into his right front pants pocket and removed an oval metallic object. "One *hand* grenade, that is."

Blade grinned, Boone laughed, and even Grizzly chuckled. Thunder stood fully erect. "I can manage on my own now."

Blade dropped his left arm to his side. "Are you sure?"

"I do not feel any dizziness or sickness," Thunder asserted. "And the weakness in my legs has passed. I can resume my duties."

"You'll take it easy for a while," Blade told him. "In fact, we'll take a ten-minute break." He walked over to the mutated bear. "I wasn't aware that black bears roamed this far south in California," he commented.

"They didn't until a few decades ago," Athena mentioned. "The bears have been extending their range southward ever since the war."

Blade nodded. "It's the same all over the country. With the human population reduced, and with nature reclaiming previously populated tracts of land, the wildlife is proliferating."

"Good!" Grizzly stated. "The less land you humans control, the less you'll screw the environment up."

"What are you talking about?" Havoc demanded.

"I know what it was like before the war," Grizzly said. "You humans had fouled up the environment with your industrial pollution, your vehicle emissions, and your aerosol sprays. Your chemical spills contaminated dozens of waterways and killed millions of fish. Your acid rains ate away at the virgin forests. Your toxic-waste dumps sickened humans and animals alike. And your kind was responsible for the extinction of dozens of species." He snorted. "You humans have a knack for fouling up everything you touch."

"You can't blame us for the mistakes of our forefathers," Boone chimed in.

"Yeah," Havoc said. "I know you don't think very highly of humans, but we have achieved some impressive accomplishments."

"That you have," Grizzly conceded sarcastically. "I was real impressed when I learned that humans almost destroyed the world. Few things have impressed me as much."

Thunder knelt and retrieved his M-16, then crossed to Grizzly. He placed his right hand on the hybrid's left shoulder. "I thank you, brother, for saving my life. I deeply regret my earlier misgivings about having you on the Force. The Spirit-in-All-Things is present in you."

Grizzly laughed. "Don't give me that religious mumbo jumbo, Thunder. I saved your hide because you're my teammate. That's all. I'd do the same for any of you dimwits."

"Not to change the subject," Athena said, "but do you think the Vampires heard the shots?"

Blade gazed to the southwest. "There's no way of telling."

"I am ready to continue," Thunder declared.

"Grizzly and Havoc, take the point," Blade ordered.

"I am fit to take the point," Thunder said.

"You'll take it easy for a while," Blade instructed him.

Grizzly knelt and wiped his claws clean on the bear's corpse. He slowly relaxed his fingers and the claws slid from sight. "I'm ready," he said, retrieving his M-16. He glanced at the noncom. "Let's go, soldier-boy. And try not to get lost."

"I don't get lost," Havoc responded indignantly.

They hastened to the southwest.

"Stay in sight!" Blade called out.

Sergeant Havoc nodded.

Blade let them go 20 yards off before hiking after them. He hefted the Commando and alertly scanned the vegetation. Where there was one wild mutant, there were probably more. Aguanga and vicinity were officially designated as a Cleared Area, an area where the California Army had exterminated most of the feral mutants.

Most.

But obviously not all.

The Force trekked on a southwesterly course throughout the afternoon and early evening hours, penetrating ever deeper into the Cleveland National Forest.

"There once was a state park around here somewhere," Athena mentioned at one point.

"Not any more?" Blade asked.

"No. People don't like to travel too close to the Dead Zone. But I remember seeing the park listed on a map. Palomar Mountain State Park was the name of it. There was a famous observatory near the peak, as I recall. The Mount Palomar Observatory," Athena detailed.

The terrain sloped gradually upwards.

Another half hour brought them to the north shore of a fair-sized lake. Grizzly and Sergeant Havoc were waiting near a large boulder.

"It's getting too dark to see the spoor," Grizzly commented as Blade approached. "Do you want us to go on?"

"No. We'll camp here for the night," Blade said. "I wouldn't want to blunder into an ambush." He surveyed the rocky shore. "No fires. We don't know how far ahead the Vampires are, and we don't want to alert them to our presence."

"They must be miles ahead of us," Athena said.

"Maybe not," Blade disputed her. "The Vampires are engaged in a forced march with thirty-seven prisoners, and they won't be able to travel any faster than the prisoners can. If we start a fire, we run the risk of having it spotted. So no fire."

"I bet I freeze my tootsies tonight," Athena groused. "Nights are chilly at this altitude in April."

"You'll survive," Blade stated. He gazed at each of them. "We'll eat jerky and drink from our canteens, then turn in. I don't want anyone drinking from this lake. The water could be contaminated. After we eat, Athena and I will take the first watch. Grizzly and Sergeant Havoc will take the second. Boone and Thunder the third. Three-hour shifts for everyone.''

"Can we tinkle, or will the noise attract the Vampires?" Grizzly inquired facetiously.

"Just don't tinkle in the lake," Blade advised. "If the water isn't polluted, we want to leave it that way."

"I'll be back," Grizzly said. He moved toward a jumbled mass of boulders 40 feet off.

Blade sat down on a flat rock and leaned the Commando on a nearby boulder. He removed his backpack.

"Mind if I join you?" Athena asked, taking a seat to his right before he could respond.

Sergeant Havoc, Boone, and Thunder took seats at the base of the large boulder.

"Do you want me to contact General Gallagher?" Boone asked.

"Not until we have something to report," Blade responded. He opened his backpack and fished inside for the packet of beef jerky. His fingers closed on the smooth plastic and he withdrew the packet.

Athena was doing the same. "How did you ever convince General Gallagher to supply us with jerky instead of rations?"

"I became accustomed to eating jerky at the Home," Blade said. "Venison jerky is a Family staple. The rations Gallagher gave us tasted like soggy, salty paper. I politely requested to receive jerky instead."

"I know you better than that," Athena remarked. "What else did you tell him?"

Blade grinned. "I mentioned noticing a herd of cattle on a ranch near our headquarters. Then I tapped my Bowies. He took the hint."

Athena laughed. "He was afraid you'd butcher the cattle yourself."

Blade unwrapped his packet and bit into a stick of jerky. The tangy meat caused his mouth to water. He chewed heartily and stared at the stars materializing in the steadily darkening sky.

Athena leaned back and viewed the celestial spectacle. "Do you ever wonder if there are other inhabited planets out there?"

"There are."

"How can you be so certain?" Athena inquired. "We don't have any proof."

"The Family Elders teach us there are many inhabited worlds," Blade stated. "How can anyone gaze at the immensity of the cosmos and believe otherwise? Take a look at our own world sometime, at the abundant life on this one puny planet. The Spirit does not intend for anyone or anything to exist in isolation."

"You're getting metaphysical on me again," Athena said. "You're a Warrior, yet you're also a philosopher. I've never met anyone quite like you."

"That's because thinking has become a dying art," Blade said. "The Elders teach each Family member to think for themselves."

"Well, Mr. Thinker, if there are beings on other worlds, then why haven't they contacted us? Some of their cultures must be more advanced than ours, capable of interstellar travel. Why haven't they shown up?"

"How do you know they haven't?" Blade responded.

"Be serious," Athena said.

"I am. How do you know these beings haven't already contacted certain people on our world? How do you know they don't select qualified individuals to serve as liaisons?" Blade asked.

"You've been reading too much science fiction," Athena cracked.

Blade shrugged and resumed eating.

"Where'd you ever get a crazy idea like that? From the Elders?" Athena probed.

The Warrior nodded.

"I'd like to meet one of the Elders sometime," Athena said. "Maybe one of them would consent to an interview for the *Times*."

Blade chewed on his jerky.

Grizzly walked toward them, his M-16 in his right hand, his backpack in his left. "Did I hear you talking about little green men from Mars?"

Athena chuckled and stood. "You and your hyper-keen

hearing! I think I'll go visit the ladies'." She strolled in the direction of several trees approximately 30 feet distant, her M-16 over her right shoulder.

"Fat lot of good my hearing did me today," Grizzly muttered as he rested his haunches on a rock. "That bear never made a peep before it attacked, and the wind was blowing the wrong way for me to detect its scent."

Blade observed a meteor streak across the heavens.

"I love the forest," Grizzly mentioned. "The animal half of me feels at home here." He sighed. "When my stint in this outfit is up, I think I'll find an uninhabited area where humans never show their ugly faces and settle down."

Blade stared at the hybrid. "Why do you pretend to dislike humans so much?"

"Who's pretending?" Grizzly rejoined archly.

"You are," Blade said. "I know you don't despise humans as much as you claim. You're friendly with us on the Force. And Athena and you are very close."

"Athena's a sweetheart," Grizzly stated. "And as for the rest of you chumps, you're not bad for meatheads. But don't get me wrong. I may like some humans, but as a species you're scum. You're a blight on this planet. The only thing I can compare humans to is a horde of locusts. You destroy everything you get your grubby mitts on."

"That's not true," Blade said. "Humans have their faults, true. But we also strive to achieve spiritual ideals. We have created great art and literature. Many humans have learned to live lives devoted to loving others. A few bad apples don't spoil the whole bunch."

"Tell me this, Bright Guy," Grizzly declared. "If your species is so great, why have humans had so many wars? Why did your kind nearly wreck the world?"

"There have always been power-mongers," Blade said. "And there have always been those who believed in using violence to achieve their ends. Humans have yet to learn how to live in harmony."

Grizzly laughed. "Now there's an understatement if I ever heard one!"

Before their conversation could continue, a horrified scream pierced the night.

# CHAPTER FIVE

"Athena!" Grizzly bellowed, and was off like a shot, heading for the trees 30 feet away, forgetting his M-16 and his backpack.

Blade scooped up his Commando but left the backpack on the ground. He sprinted toward the trees.

Thunder, Boone, and Sergeant Havoc were also coming on the run.

A pale form appeared in the trees for an instant, then was gone.

Vampires! Blade gripped the Commando firmly. He saw Grizzly plunge into the undergrowth and a moment later followed suit.

Grizzly was five yards in the lead when he abruptly stopped and leaned down.

Blade reached Grizzly's side. "What is it?"

Grizzly straightened with an M-16 in his right hand. "This is Athena's!"

Sergeant Havoc, Thunder, and Boone joined them, each one armed with their M-16s. Only Havoc had his backpack on.

"The bastards have Athena!" Grizzly hissed, exposing his

teeth and facing to the southwest. He sniffed the air noisily. "I have their scent!"

"We go after them," Blade said. "But first we get our backpacks."

"I'm not waiting!" Grizzly snapped, and took off at a fast springing gait, still holding Athena's M-16.

"Grizzly!" Blade called, to no avail.

In seconds Grizzly was lost to view.

"Damn!" Blade fumed. He glanced at Boone and Thunder. "Go get all the gear!"

They hurried toward the lake.

"How did the Vampires know we were here?" Sergeant Havoc asked.

"Who knows?" Blade replied. "Maybe they heard the shots earlier. Maybe they were checking their back trail. Maybe they have senses we don't know about."

"Want me to go after Grizzly?" Havoc offered.

"No," Blade said. "we'll stick together. Grizzly should have waited. Another minute wouldn't make a difference. We need those backpacks. They have our food and water, not to mention our plastic explosives, spare ammo, and the radio Boone's carrying." He paused. "I'm going to have a long talk with Grizzly later."

"I wouldn't want to be in Grizzly's . . ." Havoc began, about to say "shoes," then corrected himself. ". . . furry feet."

Blade waited impatiently for Boone and Thunder, chafing at every second of delay.

"The Vampires will be expecting us to come after her," Sergeant Havoc noted. "We could walk right into a trap."

"We don't have any choice," Blade said.

They waited in silence until their companions returned. Boone and Thunder were both wearing their backpacks. Boone was holding another in his left hand. Thunder held two extra backpacks and an extra M-16.

"This one is yours," Boone said to Blade.

Blade quickly aligned the backpack on his back.

"One of these backpacks is Athena's," Thunder commented. "The other gear is Grizzly's."

"We'll divide it up," Blade directed. "I'll take Grizzly's

M-16.'' He took the weapon and slung it over his left shoulder.
"Let Havoc and Boone carry the extra backpacks."

"I can carry one," Thunder said.

"Maybe later," Blade stated. "Havoc and Boone weren't
clipped by a bear today."

"I am fit," Thunder insisted.

"Later," Blade reiterated.

Boone and Havoc took the extra backpacks and slid their left
arm through the strap loops, adjusting the backpacks on their
left shoulders.

"It's a good thing we travel light," Boone quipped.

"Let's go," Blade said.

"How will we know which way to go?" Boone inquired.

"The Vampires have been heading to the southwest all day,"
Blade answered. "That's the way we'll go." He gazed up at
the stars, taking his bearings. Like the Flathead, the
Cavalryman, and Sergeant Havoc, he was adept at using the
alignment of the constellations and stars at given times of the
year as a guide for night travel. The celestial arrangement in
the California sky differed somewhat from Minnesota; he had
spent weeks after his arrival familiarizing himself with the starry
realm.

"Does this mean we don't get our beauty sleep?" Sergeant
Havoc joked.

Blade started to the southwest, his eyes constantly scanning
the landscape. The night was moonless, the countryside murky.
He moved as rapidly as the limited light and the tangled growth
allowed. Boone was behind him, then Thunder and Sergeant
Havoc.

The minutes dragged by. An hour elapsed. Two. Three.

Blade halted at the crest of a rise and surveyed the valley
below for signs of a campfire.

Nothing.

The four men pressed on.

Another hour passed.

Blade mentally debated whether to stop for the night and
resume their search in the morning or keep going. All four of
them could use some rest. The farther they went, the more
convinced he became that they would not catch up with Grizzly

and the Vampires before dawn. Even if they did, a firefight against unknown adversaries in the dark gave their enemies the edge. He preferred to tackle the Vampires during the day.

Fifteen minutes went by.

Blade emerged from the trees and found a narrow field in their path. He stopped and stared at the others. "We'll take a break here."

"Shouldn't we stay after them?" Sergeant Havoc asked in surprise.

"We need a few hours' sleep," Blade said. "We won't perform at our peak if we're exhausted. It's already past midnight. Thunder and you will grab two hours of shut-eye, then Boone and I."

"Yes, sir," Havoc responded. He immediately proceeded to lie on the ground.

"I hope you know what you're doing," Boone commented to the Warrior.

"So do I," Blade said.

Grizzly could move at an astonishingly swift pace when he wanted, and he bolted after Athena's abductors with all the speed at his command. He knew he was disobeying Blade, violating procedure, and being insubordinate, but he couldn't help himself. Athena Morris was his one true friend, and he intended to save her at all costs. Of all the humans he'd ever known, she was one of the few who looked at him without a hint of fear or revulsion in her eyes.

The Vampires would pay for taking her!

He tracked them easily, his flaring nostrils registering the unmistakable scent of the Vampires commingled with Athena's sweet womanly smell. The padded soles of his feet seldom made a noise. Leaves and limbs brushed against his fur. His fingers twitched as he envisioned slashing the Vampires to ribbons.

The trail bore to the southwest for over a mile, then inexplicably angled to the southeast, then the east.

What was this?

Why had the Vampires changed direction?

Grizzly ran at a dogtrot, bent over at the waist so he could readily distinguish the odors he was following. The Vampires, he judged, were in a hurry to get somewhere. Their scent hung in the air lightly, as if they were hastening to a definite destination.

But where?

An hour later he found the answer.

Grizzly came up over a low hill and slowed to a standstill. A quarter of a mile distant was a flickering campfire. He doubted the Vampires would light a fire and reveal their location; the fire must belong to someone else.

Who?

Grizzly descended toward the fire, advancing stealthily, craftily employing trees and thickets as cover. The woodland was exceptionally still. Not even an insect stirred.

A bad sign.

He crouched behind a broad tree trunk 40 yards from the campfire and scrutinized the area around the blaze for the slightest movement.

There was none.

Puzzled, Grizzly closed on the campfire. He was within 20 yards of the slowly diminishing flames when the breeze wafted a new scent to his nostrils.

Blood.

Fresh blood.

He held his arms at his sides, prepared to extend his claws on a second's notice, and silently padded toward the fire. Eight yards from the blaze he found a crumpled deerskin tent in a heap on the grass. Two more strides and he spied the first body.

It was a man slumped over a small log, lying on his stomach, his arms outspread, his face twisted to the side, his features locked in an expression of stark fright. Long black hair cascaded over his shoulders. He wore a brown flannel shirt and buckskin pants and moccasins.

Grizzly warily walked over to the corpse. He gingerly touched the man's left cheek and the head dropped at an unnatural angle. The man's neck was broken! Grizzly knelt and examined the victim's face closely.

The dead man was an Indian.

What had happened here?

Grizzly straightened and slowly circled the fire, finding five more bodies, all Indians. Three had died of snapped vertebrae, two of crushed throats. He speculated that the Indians had been hunting in the hills when the Vampires had waylaid them. There was no telling where the Indians hailed from. Prior to the war over a dozen Indian Reservations had existed in the general area: the Mission Indian Reservation, the Pechanga Reservation, the Rincon Reservation, Los Coyotes Indian Reservation, and many, many more. Thunder had mentioned them one night while the Force members were lounging in their barracks.

The fire light glinted off a metallic object to the right.

Grizzly crossed to the object and knelt. A Winchester was partially concealed in a clump of weeds. He picked up the weapon and sniffed the barrel. The gun had not been fired, which meant the Vampires had decimated the Indians quickly; the hapless Indians had been unable to get off so much as a single shot. He dropped the Winchester, unwilling to lug a second firearm along.

How far ahead were the Vampires?

He walked to an Indian with a pulverized throat and placed his left palm on the corpse's forehead. The skin was quite warm, and he estimated the Vampires were less than 30 minutes in front of him. With his neck tilted, he walked in ever widening circles, sniffing the air until he found the Vampire scent again. Casting a parting glance at the Indian encampment, he jogged in pursuit of the Vampires and Athena. He felt a degree of relief at not finding her body in the camp. The Vampires were still holding her prisoner, but at least she was alive.

For now.

His muscles rippling and flowing under his fur, he covered mile after mile. Fatigue nagged at his mind but he refused to acknowledge his body's complaint. He'd sleep after Athena was rescued, not before. The Vampires were again bearing to the southwest. As the hours elasped and his weariness grew and grew, his alertness lessened and lessened. His stubbornness and tenacity supplanted his better judgment and he pressed ever onward instead of resting.

Ultimately, this caused his undoing.

Grizzly followed the spoor into a rocky gorge where the Vampire scent was stronger than ever before. Had he been fully vigilant, he might have wondered why the Vampire odor was suddenly so sharp. But he jogged farther into the gorge, his wariness dulled by his strenuous exertion. Consequently, he didn't realize he was in danger until a lean, pale figure unexpectedly launched itself from a boulder on his left.

The Vampires were waiting for him!

He felt powerful arms close on his knees and he was knocked to the right. Unable to stay erect he toppled over, releasing the M-16.

Snarling, the Vampire lunged at the bear-man's neck.

Grizzly reacted instinctually, avoiding the Vampire's raking fingers and slamming his right fist into the thing's face. Dislodged by the mighty blow, the Vampire was sent rolling to one side. Grizzly heaved to his knees as the patter of onrushing feet sounded to his rear. He tried to turn.

A hurtling Vampire rammed into the bear-man from behind.

Bowled over by the impact, Grizzly found himself with his nose in the dirt and a Vampire clamping its fingers on the back of his neck. He reached over his right shoulder and gripped a cool, clammy wrist. His dense shoulder muscles straining, he wrenched on the Vampire's arm and was rewarded by the creature sailing over his head to crash into a nearby boulder.

Move your butt! his mind shrieked.

Grizzly rose to his hands and knees, intending to unsheath his lethal claws as he stood, but he never got the chance.

Three more Vampires pounced on him.

Borne to the ground by the things piling on top of him, Grizzly twisted and lashed out, striking with his fists, crunching a nose on one foe and pounding the left eye on a second.

Undaunted, the Vampires gripped his wrists, one on each arm, and held fast. The third creature, the one with the busted nose, slugged the mutant on the jaw three times in succession.

Grizzly felt his fury mounting, but he also felt uncomfortably giddy. He struggled to break free, amazed at the strength the thin, seemingly frail Vampires possessed.

Growling wickedly, the third Vampire delivered two more punches to the bear-man's chin.

Pinpoints of light were spinning before Grizzly's eyes. His eyelids fluttered as he attempted to shake off the things one final time. They were immovable. The last sound he heard was a peculiar titter.

# CHAPTER SIX

Shortly past noon.

They emerged from the forest on the bank of a stream. Thunder was in the lead, engaged in reading the sign. Blade was a few feet to his rear. Then came Boone and Sergeant Havoc.

Thunder knelt and inspected a footprint impressed in the mud at the edge of the stream. He looked up and saw the strangers. "We have company," he announced.

Blade had seen them.

Six Indians were on the opposite bank of the ribbon of water, standing 15 yards downstream. Each was armed with a rifle. They were attired primarily in buckskins, although a few cotton or wool shirts and a pair of jeans were in evidence.

Thunder stood and smiled.

The Indians whispered among themselves.

"Fan out," Blade ordered softly.

Sergant Havoc moved to the right, Boone to the left.

"I will go talk to them," Thunder offered.

"Let them come to us," Blade stated.

A heavyset Indian in buckskins slowly approached the Force

members. He nervously glanced from one to another and finally focused on Thunder. When he was directly across the stream from the Flathead, he stopped.

"Greetings, brother," Thunder said sincerely. "I am of the Flathead tribe in Montana. My parents named me Thunder-Rolling-in-the-Mountain." He grinned. "My mother believed a long name was distinctive."

The heavyset Indian smiled. "I am called Shadow. My people were once confined to the La Jolla Reservation, but we now claim this land as our own."

"We did not know this is your land," Thunder said. "We apologize if we are trespassing."

Shadow looked at the giant. "Who is your leader?"

"How do you know he is our leader?" Thunder responded.

"He has the eyes of a leader," Shadow said.

"I am Blade," the Warrior declared.

"Why are you here?" Shadow asked.

"We seek those the whites call Vampires," Thunder answered.

Shadow did a double take.

"You know of them?" Thunder questioned.

"Yes," Shadow said. "They are the scourge of my people. We call them the Blood Drinkers."

"A party of Blood Drinkers passed this way during the night," Thunder divulged. "Did you see them?"

Shadow shook his head. "You would be wise to avoid contact with them. They are death to all."

"We must find them," Thunder said. "They have taken one of us, a woman."

Shadow gazed at the stream. "The Blood Drinkers have raided my people many times and stolen many women. Our braves have tracked them to the Red Land where demons dwell. The Blood Drinkers live there."

"Have you gone into the Red Land?" Thunder inquired.

"No one may enter the Red Land and live," Shadow replied. "The demons slay all who do."

"How far are we from the Red Land?" Thunder asked.

Shadow pondered for several seconds. "From the spot where we stand, perhaps twenty miles."

"We thank you for this information," Thunder said, "and we hope we may pass through your land in peace."

"You may," Shadow stated. "And should you encounter our brothers, tell them that we are looking for them."

"Your brothers?"

"We are but half of a hunting party," Shadow disclosed. "Six of our brothers went to the east two days ago after deer. They were supposed to meet us this morning, but they did not show up at our meeting site." He paused and frowned. "I hope the Blood Drinkers did not find them."

"If we see your brothers, we will tell them we saw you," Thunder promised.

"Thank you," Shadow said. "And may the Breath Giver guide your footsteps."

"Yours as well," Thunder said.

Shadow nodded and returned to his companions. They conversed for a minute, then melted into the forest.

Boone walked to the edge of the stream. "Why didn't someone let us know that the Indians have reclaimed this land?"

"I've been wondering the same thing," Blade commented. "Surely General Gallagher or Governor Melnick must know, yet they didn't inform me."

"Maybe they don't consider it important," Thunder speculated. "What are a few tracts of land compared to the total size of California? Then again, they might not know. Not many whites live in this area. The tribes may have quietly reclaimed the land, without bloodshed."

"Let's keep going," Blade instructed.

Thunder stared to the southwest. "I fear for the safety of the missing half of that hunting party."

"Why?" Blade queried.

"Because I believe some of the Vampires have left the main column," Thunder said.

Blade's eyes narrowed. "What makes you say that?"

Thunder pointed at the mud fringing the stream. "I was not certain until we reached this spot. The Vampires do not leave many tracks, but some. All morning I found even fewer than yesterday, although the prints of the captives have been easy to read. I suspect some of the Vampires have gone a separate way. Perhaps the ones who abducted Athena last night, the ones sent to check their back trail, did not return to the prisoner column. Perhaps they went elsewhere.''

"After the other half of the hunting party?" Blade deduced.

Thunder nodded grimly. "That would be my guess."

"How many Vampires left the original group?" Blade inquired.

"It's hard to tell," Thunder said. "But not more than ten. I estimate there were three dozen or so originally."

Blade sighed in frustration. "Terrific!" he muttered. "This means Athena is not with the main column. And Grizzly is after the splinter group. They could be anywhere in the forest."

"I am sorry," Thunder apologized. "I should have noticed the exact point where the smaller group of Vampires separated. I should have said something before this."

"Don't blame yourself," Blade said. He stared at Boone and Havoc. "No breaks today. We press on until nightfall. If you get hungry, nibble on some jerky."

Thunder waded across the stream.

Blade stepped into the placid water. His apprehension was mounting by the hour. Barring a fluke, he doubted the Force would overtake the Vampires conducting the prisoners from Aguanga before the mysterious creatures reached the sanctuary of the Dead Zone. And the prospect of Athena being held by another group of Vampires who were prowling through the wilderness in search of new victims caused him intense mental anguish.

Thunder was waiting on the bank ten feet away.

Blade crossed the stream, and together they covered Boone and Sergeant Havoc as the latter two joined them. With Thunder taking point, they struck off to the southwest once again.

The afternoon hours passed slowly, uneventfully. Birds flitted through the trees. Squirrels scampered on the limbs. Rabbits darted from their path. Once a magnificent 12-point buck bounded from a thicket and disappeared to their rear.

Blade gazed at the sinking sun and reflected on the mission. They were approaching the boundary of the Dead Zone; by his calculations, they were no more than two or three miles from their destination. He was not about to go into the Dead Zone after dark. They would spend a restful night in the woods, then penetrate the Zone in the morning. He surveyed the countryside ahead for a suitable campsite.

And spied the . . . animal.

At first glance he thought it was a raccoon. The creature was perched on a log 50 feet in front of Thunder. It balanced its squat body on all fours and stared balefully at the human intruders. A coat of reddish-brown fur covered its upper body, but the color shaded to gray underneath. A bushy tail with six alternating black stripes was visible. The animal appeared to be three feet in height and in the neighborhood of 50 pounds. Blade peered at its face, bothered by an unnatural, freakish aspect to its head.

The thing spun and jumped behind the log.

Blade grinned, blaming his apprehension on a bad case of nerves. Even if the creature was a mutant, what serious harm could a mutated raccoon do to four well-armed men?

Plenty, as events developed.

Especially if the raccoon wasn't alone.

Thunder did not notice the raccoon. He was intently studying the ground for spoor when he came to a small clearing and halted.

"This looks like a good spot to camp tonight," Blade commented as he reached the clearing.

"Fine by me," Boone said. "My feet are killing me."

"You are accustomed to riding a horse," Thunder remarked.

"I wish we had horses now," Boone stated.

Sergeant Havoc, standing closest to the trees, gazed to the right. "Sir, we have company."

Blade swiveled and froze.

Three of the creatures were ten feet off, scrutinizing the Force members with cold, beady eyes. From the neck down they resembled raccoons; from the neck up they were deformed. Their heads were twice the normal size; their eyes were slanted and slightly bulbous; their foreheads protruded from their skulls; and their mouths were ringed with teeth two inches long.

"There are more over here," Boone said, staring to the left.

Blade pivoted to find five more of the things.

"There are five in front of us," Thunder stated.

Blade glanced to their rear and the hairs on the nape of his neck prickled.

Six of the creatures were behind them.

"I don't like this," Boone said softly.

And the clearing erupted in a paroxysm of bloodshed.

The creatures hissed, snarled, and screeched as they launched themselves at the humans.

Blade, poised near the middle of the clearing, tossed his Commando aside as one of the mutants sprang at him. Employing the machine gun at such close quarters would be disastrous. He would risk shooting his men accidentally. Instead, he drew his Bowies, the big knives flashing up and out. He whipped the right Bowie in a tight arc, catching the first mutant on the neck, the razor edge severing the creature's head in a crimson spray of gushing blood.

Thunder, with a clear field of fire before him, leveled his M-16 and fired as the five mutants charged him. The slugs tore into their bodies, slamming them to the grass. Convulsing in their death throes, they still attempted to reach him, to snap at his legs.

To the rear, Sergeant Havoc tried to turn and bring his M-16 into play. But six fierce forms attacked him simultaneously, leaping onto his chest and ramming into his legs. He went down.

Four of the mutants converged on Boone, two from the left, two from the right. The pair on the left missed as the Cavalryman sidestepped their rush, but the duo on the right connected, hurling themselves upward and landing on his backpack, their combined 104 pounds driving him forward onto his knees. One of them, hissing and spitting, clawed its way up and over the backpack. Boone felt a burning sensation on the rear of his head as the mutant's claws sliced his flesh. He deliberately threw himself backwards onto the ground, pinning the raccoon clinging to the backpack between the pack and the turf and upending the mutant clawing at his head. Flat on his back, exposed, and vulnerable, Boone resorted to the weapons he was a master at using.

The Cavalryman flung the M-16 to the left and drew his Hombres.

Boone rolled to the right, rising to his knees with the revolvers held at waist height. The mutant he'd pinned was three feet away, scrambling to its feet. He shot it through the head. A yard beyond were three more, between the Cavalryman and the trees. They charged him in a concerted assault, and they died in the space of a second as the Hombres thundered and belched lead. Boone twisted, and there was Blade impaling one of the mutants on the point of his left Bowie. But another raccoon was in midair, springing at the Warrior's crotch. Boone blasted the creature in the forehead and saw its brain blow out the back of its head. Out of the corner of his eye he detected movement and swiveled in time to see yet another mutant bounding toward him. With ruthless efficiency he shot the animal through the eyes.

Sergeant Havoc was still on the ground, fighting for his life, struggling and thrashing as six of the mutants tore at his body. One was tearing at his right leg, another the left. Three were on his chest and the last was striving to rend his throat. Havoc's hands were clamped on the mutant's neck and he was holding its furious form at bay.

Boone took a gamble. In a millisecond he realized Havoc's grip was slipping, that the noncom's life was on the line. With the thought came an instantaneous response; the right Hombre boomed. The impact of the 44 Magnum slug at a range of only five feet literally tore the mutant from Havoc's grasp, the slug penetrating the center of the raccoon's forehead, passing completely through its body, and bursting out its anus.

Sergeant Havoc, his hands unexpectedly free, swept both arms out and in, his hands rigid, the calloused edges connecting with one of the raccoon's on his chest, one hand just behind each ear. Blood spurted from its nostrils and ears as its neck was crushed. A second mutant snapped at his right wrist but missed. Havoc boxed the raccoon on the right ear, knocking it to the ground.

And then Blade was there, stabbing his right Bowie into the back of the mutant on the ground even as his left Bowie speared into the raccoon on Havoc's right leg.

The remaining mutant on the noncom's chest snarled and went for the human's face.

Sergeant Havoc was faster. His right hand caught the raccoon by the throat and he hoisted it into the air, his left hand thrusting against the creature's chin in a Shotei strike, a palm-heel blow. The raccoon's neck snapped with a loud crack and it slumped in his hand.

A lone raccoon was alive, the one on Havoc's left leg. It abruptly darted toward the trees.

Thunder, waiting for an unobstructed shot, fired once.

The last of the mutant raccoons screeched as it tumbled and rolled several yards, to crash against the trunk of a tree. It gasped once and expired.

The clearing was suddenly, eeerily quiet.

Blade wrenched his Bowies from the raccoons he'd slain and straightened, blood dripping from the blades.

"I always considered raccoons harmless little critters," Boone commented somberly. "I never will again."

Blade knelt alongside Havoc. "Don't move."

Sergeant Havoc rose onto his elbows. "I'm okay, sir."

"Sure you are," Blade stated. "And stop calling me 'sir.' "

Havoc's face and neck were lacerated by a dozen claw marks. His brown T-shirt was torn to shreds, the skin underneath crisscrossed with crimson slashes. The fabric on his fatigue pants had been slit open below the knees and both legs displayed gaping wounds.

Boone and Thunder stepped to the noncom's side.

"I hope those things weren't rabid," Sergeant Havoc remarked.

"I don't think they were," Blade said.

"They weren't," Thunder stated with conviction. He crouched and deposited his M-16 on the ground. "I will tend your wounds. I have medicinal herbs in my backpack."

Blade scanned the forest while wiping the Bowies on his pants. "There doesn't seem to be any more."

Boone began reloading the spent cartridges in his Hombre. "You two take care of Havoc. I'll watch out for the mutants."

Sergant Havoc tilted his neck so he could gaze backwards at the gunman. "Thanks. You saved my life there."

"You would have done the same for me," Boone said.

"That was some shooting," Havoc said, complimenting the Cavalryman. "Better than I could have done."

Boone walked to the center of the clearing. A peculiar rattling emanated from his backpack. He finished reloading the revolvers, holstered them, and unslung both the extra backpack on his left shoulder and his own. His clattered as he lowered it to the grass.

"The Spirit-in-All-Things smiled on us," Thunder mentioned as he removed a brown leather pouch from his backpack. "This could have been much worse."

"A person can't let down their guard for a second," Blade said. He slid the Bowies into their sheaths, then leaned over the noncom to examine the wounds.

"They're just scratches," Sergeant Havoc stated, sounding embarrassed by the attention.

"You let us judge how serious your injuries are," Blade said. "Yes, sir."

Blade determined the face, neck, and chest cuts were largely superficial. He inspected the right leg. A circular strip of skin approximately three inches in circumference had been bitten off, but the muscles and tendons were untouched. The left leg was another story. Two inches below the knee was a ragged, four-inch strip where the skin and the muscle had been chewed off, exposing the bone. "Can you bend your left leg?" he asked.

Sergeant Havoc slowly lifted the leg, then flexed it gingerly until the leg was bent at the knee. "No problem," he said.

"Lay it down," Blade advised.

Havoc complied.

"We have a problem here," Boone interjected.

Blade glanced at the Cavalryman. "What?"

Boone was squatting with his backpack open between his legs. He reached into the pack and withdrew their radio. Their shattered radio. Wires and broken circuit boards dangled from the fractured casing. "It must have happened when I landed on my back."

"So much for contacting General Gallagher for support," Blade remarked.

Thunder pulled a small glass jar from the brown pouch, unscrewed the cap, and inserted two fingers. A greenish-blue sticky substance caked his fingers when he extracted them.

"What's that?" Sergeant Havoc asked.

"A remedy of my own," Thunder said. He started applying the ointment to the noncom's neck and face, rubbing the substance over the slash marks.

Havoc scrunched up his nose. "Whew! It stinks! What's in it?"

Thunder answered as he administered the medicine. "Ground roots and certain leaves. Bear fat. Mineral water. Eye of a newt. The toe of a frog. Bat wool. And the tongue of a dog. All the usual."

Sergeant Havoc's mouth dropped. "You're kidding, right?"

"Am I?" Thunder answered with a grin.

"You've *got* to be kidding!" Havoc insisted.

"Did I mention it also contains lizard's leg?" Thunder asked with a straight face.

# CHAPTER SEVEN

**H**e came awake slowly, his chin throbbing, a dull ache pervading his lower face. His body swayed from side to side, and he received the impression that he was being carried.

The Vampires hadn't killed him!

Why not?

Grizzly opened his eyes to find the sky filled with stars. He must have been unconscious only a short while! His eyes narrowed as he pereceived he was tied to a long, stout pole or limb. His wrists and ankles were bound securely. Craning his neck, he dicovered a Vampire bearing the front of the pole upon its left shoulder. He glanced to the rear and observed another Vampire effortlessly supporting the other end. Both wore dark loincloths.

Where were they taking him?

"So? Sleeping Beauty is awake!" the Vampire to the rear commented in a high-pitched voice, then tittered.

Grizzly recalled having heard that titter before. "You can talk!" he declared.

"No shit, Sherlock!" the Vampire said sarcastically. "You must be a genius!"

Grizzly shook his head, wondering if he was dreaming.

"Don't you have the usual zillion-and-one questions?" the Vampire inquired.

"Who are you? *What* are you?" Grizzly asked.

The Vampire sighed. "How original!"

"Where's Athena, you slime-bucket?" Grizzly demanded angrily.

"Athena?" the Vampire repeated.

"You scumbags grabbed her earlier tonight," Grizzly said. "About an hour or so before you killed six Indians."

"Earlier tonight?" the Vampire stated, and tittered. "You mean last night. You were out cold all day."

All day! Grizzly gazed at the stars again.

"You're lucky," the Vampire said. "If you were human, you'd be dead right now. We would have wasted your ass after we jumped you." He paused. "But we've never seen anyone like you before. Loring thinks we should take you to Corpus."

"Where's Athena?" Grizzly repeated belligerently.

"Is that the bitch's name?" the Vampire responded. "She's with the rest of the foodstuff. We rejoined the others a while ago."

Foodstuff? Grizzly stared at the Vampire. "Do you have a name?"

"Polidori, at your service," the Vampire said in a mocking tone.

"What the hell are you?" Grizzly snapped.

"The humans call us Vampires," Polidori said. "They've been calling us that for years."

"What do you call yourselves?" Grizzly asked.

"The Venesects," Polidori replied.

"Where are you taking me?"

"You'll see," Polidori said.

"What do you plan to do with me?" Grizzly probed.

Polidori tittered. "You'll see."

"I see I'd like to cram that smirk down your throat!" Grizzly declared testily.

"You're not the timid type," Polidori commented. "I like that. It means you have good blood. I think I'll put in dibs."

Dibs? "I want to see Athena," Grizzly stated.

Polidori grinned. "Don't hold your breath."

"I'll remember you when I get free," Grizzly threatened.

"I'm scared to death," Polidori quipped. He stared skyward for several seconds. "We'll reach the Heartland before daylight. Perfect! I won't need to spend another day curled up under some rotten tree."

"You camp during the day and travel at night," Grizzly deduced. "Why?"

"Wouldn't you like to know," Polidori responded.

Grizzly, feeling supremely frustrated, scowled. He'd rate his performance on the mission as less than zero. He was separated from Blade and the others. He had failed to rescue Athena. Worse yet, he'd allowed himself to be captured by a bunch of pasty wimps! He needed to redeem himself, and as he saw it, there were two options. The ropes binding him to the pole were tight, but he knew he could break loose if he applied all of his prodigious strength. Freeing himself, though, was not the wisest course; he was outnumbered, and he did not know Athena's exact location. Since he wouldn't escape without taking her, his other option was to wait for the right moment, to let the Vampires, or the Venesects as they called themselves, take him to the Heartland.

"Do you have any idea how many pints of blood are in your body?" Polidori unexpectedly asked.

"No. Why?" Grizzly responded.

"I was just wondering about the divvy," Polidori answered.

"What's the divvy?" Grizzly questioned.

"Bits and pieces. Pieces and bits," Polidori said and laughed.

Grizzly wanted to wring Polidori's skinny neck. He calmed his boiling temper, holding his emotions in check until the proper time.

Polidori would get his, eventually.

Grizzly intended to see to it personally.

# CHAPTER EIGHT

"So this is the San Diego Dead Zone," Boone remarked, sounding utterly unimpressed. "It doesn't look much different from the Dead Zone I saw in the Dakota Territory five years ago."

They were standing on a low hill 50 yards from the Dead Zone. The contrast between the Zone and the prolific vegetation in the forest was startling. The forest was lush and green, the Zone was devoid of plant life. The forest soil was rich in nutrients and a healthy brown, but the Dead Zone earth was parched and reddish.

"It looks like a red desert," Sergeant Havoc mentioned.

"This place is evil," Thunder said solemnly. "A violation of Nature."

Blade scanned the red dunes for a sign of life. Not so much as an insect stirred. "Somewhere in there is where we'll find the Vampires. Does everyone have a full canteen?"

"Yes, sir," Havoc said.

"Mine is full," Thunder replied.

"Same here," Boone stated.

Blade looked at the noncom. "Are you sure you're up to this?

You can wait here for us to return."

"No way, sir," Havoc asserted. "I've come this far. I'll go all the way."

"Suit yourself," Blade said. "Head on out! Thunder, take the point. No more than ten yards in front. I'll bring up the rear."

They advanced to the edge of the Dead Zone and halted.

"There," Thunder said, pointing. "Following them will be easy."

The surface of the fine red dirt was marked by dozens of footprints, all heading to the west.

"Keep your eyes peeled," Blade advised. He waited as the others marched into the Zone, then trudged after them. He scrutinized Sergeant Havoc.

The noncom walked with a pronounced limp. Thunder had treated and bandaged both legs, thereby preventing infection. By all rights Havoc should be recuperating in a bed. The strain of the prolonged hiking waas aggravating his wounds. He could not apply all of his weight to his left leg, and he hobbled on his left foot as he proceeded gamely into the Zone.

A mile was traversed in silence. The montony of the barren terrain was oddly oppressive, seeming to radiate an aura of menace.

"This place is creepy," Boone commented as they crested a dune.

Ahead was a flat expanse of red earth.

"I hear there are Dead Zones all over the country," Sergeant Havoc said. "All kinds of monsters inhabit them."

"Just what I wanted to hear," Boone cracked.

Blade noticed a mound of red dirt to their right and 40 feet in front of them. The mound was S-shaped, five feet high, and over 20 in length.

They tramped half the distance to the mound.

Blade felt perspiration beading his forehead. The sun, strangely, was baking his skin, as if the red earth served as an oven, reflecting and amplifying the heat. He mopped at his brow with his right hand. How could anything live in such a land? he wondered. How did the Vampires survive and thrive under such harsh, arid circumstances?

Sergeant Havoc glanced over his left shoulder. "It's hard to believe this was once a major city, isn't it, sir?"

"I asked you to stop calling me sir," Blade reminded the noncom. "Blade will do."

"I've spent my adult life calling my superiors sir," Havoc noted. "It's hard to break old habits."

Blade gazed absently at the mound of dirt, then at the far horizon. "Have you ever been in a Dead Zone before?"

"No," Sergeant Havoc admitted.

"I was in New York City once," Blade divulged. "There was red dirt and molten slag everywhere." He paused. "New York City had a population of fifteen to twenty million when the war broke out. Fifteen to twenty million lives were obliterated in mere minutes. It's difficult to appreciate the reality of such total destruction. Here we are, walking where a major city once stood. What was San Diego's population? Close to two million?" He shook his head. "I still can't seem to fully grasp the magnitude of the war."

"I know what you mean," Sergeant Havoc said.

"Every time I think of the war, and of our ancestors, I keep coming back to the same question," Blade stated. "How could they do this to themselves?"

"And what's the answer?" Sergeant Havoc responded.

"The Family Elders teach a course called The History of World War Three," Blade said. "It's very interesting. World War Three, they say, was the result of several factors. One was the absolute incompatibility of capitalism and communism. Capitalism was based on the profit motive and the private ownership of property, while communism vested all ownership in the state and held all property in common. The two systems were diametrically opposed. And the communists were intolerant of other political beliefs. They wanted to rule the world. The man who wrote *The Communist Manifesto*, Karl Marx, stated their goal plainly. He advocated the forcible overthrow of all existing social conditions."

"What other factors were involved?" Sergeant Havoc asked.

"The military factor was one," Blade detailed. "Both sides constantly strived to hold the edge militarily. They poured billions of dollars into ever newer and better weapons systems.

If they had spent half of that money on their social problems, like poverty and illiteracy, they could have cured their social ills. But each side was determined to be King of the Mountain. They perfected the art of war until it became racially suicidal. Their leaders tried to achieve peace through diplomacy and treaties. They failed because neither side trusted the other, they misled each other, and because promises and pledges are no substitute for a genuine craving for peace.''

Sergeant Havoc absorbed the Warrior's words thoughtfully.

''Another factor was the spiritual one,'' Blade went on. ''In America the people were free to worship as they pleased. There was religious diversity, although the secular humanists tried to mold a society without a spiritual foundation. On the Russian side, the government, the Communist Party, was officially and actively atheistic. They considered religious beliefs a form of insanity. A godless society can never coexist with a religious one.''

Havoc stared at the ground. He was amazed at the Warrior's analysis. What manner of men and women did they raise in the Family? How could Blade be such a skilled fighter, and so ruthless when necessary, and yet be so philosophical—indeed spiritual—at the same time? He did not understand.

The Force members passed within six feet of the mound of S-shaped dirt.

Blade gazed idly at the mound as they strolled by. He noticed the granular texture of the dirt, and the particles shimmering in the sunlight.

They were ten feet beyond the mound when Thunder abruptly halted and crouched, his right hand feeling the impressions at his feet. He looked back at Blade. ''They are carrying someone.''

''Be specific,'' Blade directed.

''Two of the Vampires are leaving clear footprints,'' Thunder explained. ''Their feet are sinking deeper in the dirt. Either they are fat Vampires, or they are bearing additional weight. They are walking about seven feet apart. I think they are carrying someone or something between them, probably using a branch.''

Sergeant Havoc's mind flashed back to their first mission, the strike against the vile Spider. ''The Hatchlings transported me that way after I was caught."

"Is there any indication the Vampires wear shoes or boots?" Blade inquired.

"None," Thunder responded. "All I've seen are prints of naked feet. Their soles must be solid callus.

"How much of a lead do they have?" Blade queried.

Thunder studied the tracks for a moment. "These tracks were made during the night. It's ten o'clock now. I'd say they passed here about four in the morning."

"Maybe we can catch up with them before nightfall," Blade stated hopefully. "Head out."

They resumed their trek into the Dead Zone.

Blade took several strides, then stopped, listening. A weird sort of swishing had sounded for a second or two. He cocked his head and surveyed the Dead Zone on both sides.

Nothing.

Shrugging, the Warrior followed his companions.

The swishing was repeated.

Blade halted.

The swishing ceased.

Was the blistering heat affecting his hearing? Blade slowly turned, scrutinizing the alien landscape. He saw the mound, and the expanse of red earth, and . . .

The mound!

Blade's gray eyes narrowed, his grip on the Commando tightening. The mound had moved! It was no longer S-shaped, but had mysteriously straightened at one end. The end nearest the Force. He stared at the mound for over a minute, waiting for it to move again.

"Is something wrong, sir?" Sergeant Havoc called out.

Blade glanced over his right shoulder. Havoc and the others were waiting for him 50 feet away. He double-checked the mound, which displayed no hint of movement. "I guess not," he yelled. He faced westward and headed for his companions. Perhaps he had misjudged the original shape of the mound. After all, mounds of dirt did not move by themselves. There must be a logical explanation. He gazed at the others and froze.

Sergeant Havoc, Boone, and Thunder were gaping at him in stunned amazement.

No.

Not at him.

*Behind* him!

Blade whirled, his skin crawling with goose bumps at the sight he beheld.

The mound was moving, the rear portion uncurling into a straight line. And suddenly the mound performed an equally incredible feat; it started toward the Warrior.

Bewildered, Blade pressed the Commando stock against his right shoulder. He squinted to reduce the glare as insight washed over him. The mound wasn't moving: something was coming at him *under the ground!* There was something underneath the surface, something alive, something five feet in height and over 20 feet long.

Dear Spirit! What could it be?

"Blade!" Boone shouted in alarm. "Run for it!"

Blade wasn't about to run. He stood between the thing and his men, and he intended to stop whatever-it-was before it reached them. He saw the red earth ripple as the thing gained speed, the fine grains flowing up and over the thing as if the ground was pliable putty instead of dense dirt.

"Blade!" Sergeant Havoc yelled.

Blade let the thing get within five feet of him before he opened fire, the Commando thundering and bucking in his arms. The slugs smacked into the ground at the leading edge of the thing, dirt flying everywhere.

Whatever-it-was never missed a beat. The front end swerved, bearing to the left and skirting the Warrior.

Blade poured a withering burst into the side of the thing, but it was apparently unaffected.

In a burst of speed the underground denizen bypassed the giant and angled toward Sergeant Havoc.

"Havoc! Look out!" Blade bellowed and took off in pursuit.

Segeant Havoc cradled his M-16 and awaited the thing. His injured left leg precluded any hope of avoiding the behemoth. He opted to make a stand where he stood.

The thing bore down on the noncom with astonishing swiftness.

Pounding after it, Blade knew he could not reach Havoc in time. The noncom would be on his own.

Not quite.

Thunder and Boone raced around Havoc, Thunder on the left, Boone the right. They intentionally put themselves in the creature's path, running 15 feet from the noncom, then stopping.

The behemoth came on like a burrowing express train.

Thunder and Boone fired in unison, their M-16s chattering, their shots plowing into the dirt welling up over the creature's back.

The thing never slowed.

Thunder and Havoc were four feet apart when the behemoth passed between them, the ground tilting crazily and cresting like a wave in the ocean. Both lost their footing and were upended.

Blade, sweat caking his body, the blood pounding in his temples, watched in horror as the creature closed on Sergeant Havoc.

# CHAPTER NINE

General M.A. Gallagher was in no mood for interruptions. He stood in the Communications Center at March Air Force Base and glared at the hapless Communications Specialist seated in a chair before him. "I don't care if you've tried a hundred times," he snapped. "You'll keep trying until I tell you otherwise. You got that, Sergeant?"

The soldier gulped and nodded. He swiveled his chair and applied himself to the radio once more. "Bravo-Lima-Alfa-Delta-Echo, this is Big Bad Wolf. Do you copy? Over."

General Gallagher listened to the sergeant, frowning in annoyance. The Freedom Force should have radioed in a position fix at dawn. The ramifications of their failure upset him immensely. If Blade didn't call in soon, he would have to send a platoon of Rangers after the Force.

A young lieutenant approached the general. "Sir, you've been here for hours without a break. Would you care for a cup of coffee or some food?"

Gallagher looked at the lieutenant, his brown eyes narrowing. With his jowly features, stocky body, and crew-cut brown hair, he resembled a pit bull about to bite. "When I'm hungry,

Lieutenant, I'll let you know," he declared testily.

"I just meant—" the lieutenant began.

"I know exactly what you meant!" General Gallagher said, cutting him off. "You just attend to your duties and let me worry about my stomach."

The lieutenant blanched. "Yes, sir." He did an about-face and hurried off.

Gallagher clasped his hands behind his back and stared at the Communications Specialist. "Anything, Sergeant?"

"No, sir."

"Keep trying," Gallagher ordered. He glanced at a blue telephone on the wall to his left, wondering when Governor Melnick would call to inquire about the status of the mission. As the personal liaison between the Force and the governor, he, ultimately, would be praised or criticized depending on how the Force performed. So long as the Force accomplished each mission, he was content to bask in the limelight and savor the attendant benefits to his career. But if the Force failed, if Blade and company bought the farm, Gallagher knew his career might suffer. Governor Melnick, for one, would be extremely unhappy. Not to mention all of the other Federation leaders. A stigma would be attached to his sterling service record, and through no fault of his own. Sure, he'd withheld certain information pertaining to the damn Vampires from Blade. Yes, he'd deceived the Warrior, but Blade would have turned down the mission, would have refused to leave until the Force rested from their Oregon foray if Gallagher had told the complete truth. He'd deliberately given the Warrior the misimpression that the assignment in Aguanga would be a quick in-and-out affair, knowing full well that Blade's sense of dedication would take care of the rest.

Who could have figured Blade would fail?

The thick steel door to the Communications Center opened and in walked a major, a thin man with gray streaks in his hair. He crossed to the general and stood at attention. "Sir! There's someone here to see you."

General Gallagher scowled. "Not now, Major Donovan! Can't you see I'm busy?"

"Sir, this can't be helped," Major Donovan persisted.

"There's someone here to see you who came in on the courier run."

"The courier run?" Gallagher repeated, his thick eyebrows arching.

"Yes, sir," Donovan confirmed. "One of the VTOLs returned from its courier run to Minnesota fifteen minutes ago with an unexpected passenger."

Gallagher's forehead creased in perplexity. When the VTOLs weren't required to shuttle the Force on a mission, they were utilized as a courier service between the Federation factions. The jets did not ferry passengers on a regular basis, except for Blade. The Warrior visited the Home at least once a month. "Who was the pilot?"

"Captain Laslo," Major Donovan answered.

"I'll bust him down to airman for breaking regulations!" Geneal Gallagher stated.

"You'll do nothin' of the kind, honky," said a low, firm voice from the doorway.

General Gallagher pivoted, his mouth slackening. "You!" he blurted.

"Yeah, me," said the newcomer. "Long time no see." He sauntered into the ComCenter with an air of indifferent arrogance, a huge black man with a curly Afro attired in a brown leather vest and faded brown corduroy pants.

"Bear!" General Gallagher exclaimed.

"None other," Bear stated, stepping over to the officer.

"We haven't seen each other since the summit meeting in January," Gallagher noted. "What are you doing here?"

"Can't you guess?" Bear rejoined.

Gallagher reflected for a minute. Bear was from the Federation faction known at the Clan. They lived in the town of Halma, not far from the Family, and their leader was a man named Zahner. Bear was Zahner's right-hand man. He was also a close friend of Blade's.

"Did you figure it out yet?" Bear asked.

"I think so," Gallagher said. "You've volunteered to represent the Clan on the Force. The last man they sent didn't last very long."

Bear nodded at the rows of ribbons adorning the general's

jacket. "Is one of those for smarts? You're right on the money."

"Why did Zahner send you?" Gallagher queried. "You're one of the top Clansmen."

"So? Rank doesn't have any privileges in the Clan," Bear said. "We've all got to serve however we can."

"Blade will be delighted to see you," General Gallagher predicted.

Bear smiled. "Where is he anyway? I want to report to him right away."

General Gallagher coughed. "I'm afraid that's not possible."

"Why not?" Bear demanded, folding his muscular arms across his wide chest.

"Blade isn't here," Gallagher revealed. "He's on a mission and I don't know when he'll be back."

"Where is this mission?" Bear inquired.

"That's confidential information," General Gallagher replied brusquely.

Bear's lips compressed and he leaned forward until his nose was almost touching the officer's. His brown eyes were flinty, and his tone when he spoke was hard. "You listen to me, General, and you listen good!" he said so only Gallagher could hear. "I didn't think much of your scuzzy butt when I was in California for the summit, and I can see that you ain't changed much. You can take all those medals you're wearin' and stuff 'em up your ass! They don't mean squat to me." He paused. "I volunteered for the Force because I happen to like Blade. And I just flew two thousand miles to see him. Now you tell me where he is, or in front of all your troops I'm going to turn you upside down and shake you until you rattle. Got me?"

General Gallagher's face did a marvelous imitation of a beet. His lips worked but no words came out.

"And don't try to pull rank on me," Bear warned. "I'll take my orders from Blade and no one else. If you don't like it, you're welcome to try and do something about it."

Gallagher finally found his voice. "No one talks to me like that!" he hissed. "No one!"

"I said my piece," Bear stated. "What happens next is up to you."

Gallagher suppressed his fury with a monumental effort. He

refused to lose his control in front of subordinates.

"Where is Blade?" Bear repeated.

Gallagher knew that Bear would carry through with his threat. He knew Governor Melnick would frown on an altercation between a top-ranking officer and a lowly grunt. Tact was called for. "Blade is on a mission in the vicinity of San Diego."

"Where exactly?" Bear questioned.

"I don't know, exactly," General Gallagher confessed.

Bear gazed at the banks of communications and computer equipment lining the walls of the ComCenter. "Do you take me for a fool, honky? I may have been raised in the Twin Cities and spent most of my life in a gang, but I'm not stupid. Blade has told me a little about the Force. They always take a radio along, don't they?"

"Yes," General Gallagher verified.

"Then you must know where he is," Bear observed.

Gallagher placed his hands on his hips. "I'll be honest with you—"

"Don't change your personality on my account," Bear said, interrupting.

"I really don't know where Blade is at this moment," General Gallagher continued, ignoring the insult. "We've lost contact with the Force."

"Why don't you send in a backup unit?" Bear suggested.

"I was going to wait a while longer," Gallagher replied.

"Screw waiting," Bear stated. "I'll go after them."

General Gallagher pretended to stare at the floor to disguise his sudden grin of satisfaction. Bear's arrival could be a blessing in disguise. If he sent Bear after Blade, and if Bear failed, then the onus, the discredit, would be on Bear's shoulders. Gallagher nearly laughed. He would be off the hook!

"What about it?" Bear prompted. "Give me some men and I'll find Blade for you."

General Gallagher adopted a contemplative expression, as if he was mulling over the proposition. "I don't know," he hedged.

"Come on!" Bear goaded. "I can do it."

"It would be risky," General Gallagher commented.

"I don't care," Bear stated. "Blade is my friend, and I know Boone real well. They may be in trouble."

Gallagher scratched his chin. "Would you be willing to lead a company of Rangers into the field?"

"When do we leave?" Bear responded eagerly.

General Gallagher smiled. "In an hour. I'll order choppers to airlift you to Aguanga. You'll be on your own from there."

"Aguanga?" Bear said.

"The name of the town the Force was sent to," Gallagher divulged. "You can pick up their trail at the town."

"Looks like I owe you one," Bear said.

"I'm just doing my job," Gallagher remarked.

Bear gazed around the Communications Center. "I can use a bite to eat before I go."

"There's a mess hall outside this building and to the east," Gallagher said.

Bear turned toward the doorway.

"Wait,' Gallagher declared. "There's something I'm curious about."

Bear looked back at the general. "Like what?"

"Where did you ever get the name Bear?" General Gallagher inquired. "It's not a typical, everyday name."

"I picked it up in the Twin Cities," Bear detailed. "I belonged to a gang headed by a scumbag named Maggot. He got his kicks by givin' everybody a nickname, and the nickname he gave me stuck. Everyone has been callin' me Bear for years."

"What's your real name?" General Gallagher asked.

"What's the diff?" Bear responded. "I like my nickname better."

"I was just curious," General Gallagher said. "What is your real name?"

Bear's sheepish response was barely audible. "Harold."

# CHAPTER TEN

Sergeant Havoc stood his ground, aimed the M-16, and fired. His rounds stitched into the wave of red dirt surging toward him and the creature underneath swerved to the left, circling him. Havoc emptied the M-16's magazine in the roiling earth.

Blade raced to the noncom's aid. He saw Boone and Thunder scrambling to their feet.

The thing swung toward Havoc again the moment the M-16 went empty. He shuffled backwards, discarding the M-16 and drawing the Colt automatics.

Red dirt started spraying upwards a few feet in front of the noncom, forming a geyser of shimmering particles. The fountain of fine earth rose a full ten feet into the air, choking the air with dust and restricting visibility.

Blade spied a bulky, dark shape rising from the ground at the base of the geyser. The behemoth was emerging from its subterranean domain! "Havoc!" he shouted. "Look out! It's coming up!"

Sergeant Havoc was holding his left Colt in front of his eyes to block the swirling dirt. He squinted at the snakelike form flowing from the hole in the ground. The dust prevented him from seeing the thing clearly. Where was its head? Its eyes? Where was the monster most vulnerable?

The thing arced six feet above the ground, then its front end lunged at the noncom.

Sergeant Havoc threw himself to the right. Something smacked against his legs and he was thrown for a loop. He landed on his back facing eastward, the creature to his rear.

"Roll!" Blade bellowed.

Havoc automatically rolled to the left and something thudded onto the earth in the spot he'd just vacated. He heaved to his right knee and swiveled to confront his adversary.

And what an adversary!

The behemoth was a wormish creature of gigantic proportions, with a girth of four feet and a length five times as great. Its body was brownish-black, laced with narrow folds in the outer skin, and reeking with a sickeningly sweet odor. Headless and eyeless, the worm did possess an enormous, hideous maw consisting of reddish lips and a toothless mouth wide enough to swallow a man in one gulp.

Havoc blasted away with the Colts, a clear fluid spurting from the creature every time he hit home.

Boone and Thunder joined in, their M-16's chattering in unison.

The worm reared higher, swinging its mouth in the direction of this new threat.

And then Blade was there, on Havoc's right, the Commando in the Warrior's right hand, Grizzly's M-16 in his left. He fired them simultaneously, his massive arms absorbing the recoil.

The worm jerked and whipped its body from side to side, its maw opening and closing spasmodically.

Blade unexpectedly ceased firing, dropped the Commando and the M-16, and unslung his backpack.

Sergeant Havoc, Boone, and Thunder poured it on, the Cavalryman and the Flathead ejecting spent magazines and inserting fresh ones in a twinkling.

Havoc expended the last round in his Colts and grabbed for a new clip in his left front pocket. He saw Blade charge the worm. The Warrior was holding his right arm aloft, a packet of plastic explosive outfitted with a timer clutched in his hand.

"Me! Take me!" Blade yelled.

The worm reared up, then plunged its giant mouth toward the Warrior.

Blade heaved the explosive, a perfect toss, the packet sailing straight into the creature's maw and down its throat. "Hit the dirt!" he commanded, then flung himself from the behemoth.

The sensation of swallowing a foreign object had caused the worm to recoil skyward. It was framed against the backdrop of blue sky when the detonator went off.

Sergeant Havoc, in the act of flattening as the explosive occurred, was slammed to the earth by the concussion. Grisly chunks of brown, fleshy gore spattered all over him and the surrounding ground. He hugged the dirt, his back becoming clammy from the worm's sticky fluid raining down. His ears began ringing.

In the aftermath of the explosion the Dead Zone was preternaturally still.

"Is it dead?" Boone asked.

Sergeant Havoc looked up. Blade was rising. Thunder and Boone were already erect.

"It's dead," Blade stated.

The upper third of the worm had been blown to smithereens, leaving a jagged fringe of flesh that was oozing fluid. Its colossal body was twitching. Tendrils of smoke wafted upward.

Havoc slowly stood, brushing the dust from his clothing. "How long was the timer set for?" he inquired, glancing at the Warrior.

"Less than a minute," Blade replied.

Havoc whistled. "You believe in cutting it close!"

"There was no time to lose," Blade said.

Sergeant Havoc scrutinized the worm's repulsive corpse. "And what if you had missed?"

"I would have kept my fingers crossed for a giant robin to show up," Blade joked.

Thunder walked over to the worm, his mouth downturned. "Will we encounter more abominations like this?"

"Probably," Blade answered. "Unless we're very lucky."

Thunder surveyed the Dead Zone. "This land is a blight on Creation. I do not like being here."

"Who does?" Blade retorted. He retrieved the Commando and the M-16, reloaded both, then slung the M-16 over his left shoulder.

Segeant Havoc recovered his M-16.

"Are you okay?" Blade asked the noncom.

"No worse than before," Havoc replied.

"Then let's move out," Blade directed them.

They resumed their trek into the Dead Zone, walking in silence, alert for another attack. Hours passed and none came.

"How large is this Dead Zone?" Boone queried loudly at one point.

"Twenty miles in diameter," Sergeant Havoc answered. "At least, that's what I was told a few years ago."

Blade gazed at the red dirt. "Some cities were more fortunate than San Diego," he commented.

Boone looked back. "How so?"

"San Diego sustained a direct surface burst," Blade explained. "Other cities were hit by air bursts."

"What's the difference between the two?" Boone inquired.

"The surface burst is far more destructive and deadly," Blade said. "The blast sucks up tons and tons of dirt and debris, all of which becomes coated with radioactive material in the mushroom cloud. All of these radioactive particles then fall back to the ground, producing the fallout. So from a surface burst there are two devastating consequences. The first is the blast itself, and the area it destroys will depend on the size of the thermonuclear device. The second is the radioactive fallout, which the winds can spread over a wide area."

"The results aren't the same with an air burst?" Boone asked.

"No," Blade said. "The air burst won't destroy as large an area as the surface burst. And the air burst produces very little fallout because the blast takes place in the atmosphere above the target. Hardly any dirt or debris is drawn up into the mushroom cloud. In later years, this means less contamination of the soil."

Boone surveyed the red plain ahead. "Is this area radioactive?"

"Only slightly," Blade responded. "General Gallagher and I were discussing the war about three weeks ago. He told me the Hot Spots in California are monitored regularly. The radiation level here is higher than normal, but it's not life-threatening.''

''That's a relief,'' Boone remarked.

Thunder abruptly stopped and pointed to the west. ''What is that?''

The Force members clustered around the Flathead.

''It looks spooky,'' Boone mentioned.

Blade had to agree. A half mile off was a solitary spire rearing heavenward.

I can't make out details,'' Sergeant Havoc said.

''Let's go see what it is,'' Blade proposed, taking the lead.

They traversed a quarter of a mile, expectantly fingering their weapons.

Blade was the first to see the rim. He ascended a dune and blinked rapidly at the vista before him, astonished.

The very earth seemed to fall away not 20 yards distant. Beyond was a tremendous crater stretching as far as the eye could discern. Inside the crater was a titanic jumble of molten slag, twisted and rusted girders, ruined buildings, and heaps of rubble.

Blade walked to the crater rim and stared at the tangle of metal and stone.

''Will you look at that!'' Boone exclaimed.

''I never imagined. . . .'' Sergeant Havoc began, then stopped.

Thunder's lips compressed as he scrutinized the crater. A look of ineffable sadness etched his features.

Blade gazed at the spire, actually all that was left of a once-mighty skyscraper. The scene vividly reminded him of New York City.

''Are we going down there?'' Boone questioned. He did not sound too keen on the idea.

''Afraid so,'' Blade said. ''We know the Vampires have their lair in the Dead Zone. Where else could it be?'' He studied the slope below the rim. ''The incline is gradual. We won't have any problems getting down there.''

''It's not getting down I'm concerned about,'' Boone said. ''It's getting back up.''

"Since when did you become such a big worrywart?" Sergeant Havoc inquired.

"Ever since I signed up for the Force," Boone replied. "I miss Dakota and I want to see it again someday."

"You will," Blade assured the Cavalryman.

Boone chuckled. "Not at the rate we're going."

Blade stepped onto the slanting crater wall. The rim was only 15 yards from the bottom and he reached the base with ease. As the others slowly descended the slope, with Sergeant Havoc gingerly applying pressure to his left foot, he studied the ruins.

From the crater rim the molten slag, ravaged buildings, girders, and other debris had appeared as a packed, almost solid mass. But closer inspection revealed a maze of openings and passageways penetrating into the gloomy bowels of the ruins. Red dust caked everything. The air was hot and motionless.

"Why do I have the feeling I'm being watched?" Boone queried as the others joined the Warrior.

"I have the same feeling," Sergeant Havoc said.

"I'll go first," Blade proposed.

"Be my guest," Boone quipped.

Blade took four strides toward the ruins.

"Look!" Thunder suddenly blurted.

Everyone froze in midstride.

"What is it?" Boone asked, his eyes darting every which way.

"I saw something move," Thunder said.

Blade scanned the devastation. "Where?"

Thunder pointed at a wide opening in a 40-foot pile of rubble. "There."

"Did you get a good look at it?" Blade inquired.

"No," Thunder answered. "It was big and green. That's all I can tell you."

"How big?" Boone interjected.

"About as big as a horse," Thunder responded.

"Uh-oh," Boone said. "Here we go again."

Blade held the Commando next to his waist and advanced to the edge of the ruins. To his left rose a column of slag and to his right a shattered concrete wall.

Sergeant Havoc came next, then Boone and Thunder.

"I should have known better," Boone muttered. "When

Kilrane asked me to volunteer for the Force, I should have known better.''

"Kilrane?" Havoc repeated.

"The leader of the Cavalry," Boone detailed. "One of my best friends. He asked me to volunteer as a personal favor to him.''

Sergeant Havoc grinned. "Some friend you've got there."

"I think the next time I see him," Boone whispered, "I'll pop him in the chops."

Blade entered the ruins.

"Here goes nothing," Sergeant Havoc said, and followed.

Blade proceeded cautiously. The bizarre jungle of metal and stone was emotionally unsettling. He remembered reading about the astronauts and their flights to the moon and elsewhere, and he wondered if the space travelers had experienced similar reactions as they walked upon a totally foreign world. The passage he was on wound ever deeper into the demolished metropolis. Spires, slag, crumbling walls, and vestiges of decimated structures towered overhead. Murky shadows enveloped the landscape. A maze of passageways branched in all directions. He glanced down at the path and halted.

There, outlined by the layer of red dust, was the imprint of a naked foot.

Blade lifted his eyes and discovered a whole series of footprints heading in the direction the Force was going.

The others also noticed.

"Vampire tracks," Thunder stated.

Blade continued onward. After 50 feet he reached a junction and stopped.

The footprints bore to the left.

The Warrior pursed his lips, debating whether to stick with the tracks or take another route.

From above the Force a distinct clicking sounded.

Blade tilted his head and stared upward, searching the crevices and obscure recesses.

Again the noise was heard, a grating click-click-click. Only louder.

"It's coming toward us," Thunder commented.

A misty shower of red dust sprinkled over them.

Blade looked around and spied a section of wall 15 yards to the left. The jagged wall was five feet high and twice that in length. "On me," he declared, jogging toward the promising shelter.

Just as a gigantic, squat form dropped from the upper recesses and landed between the Force and the wall.

# CHAPTER ELEVEN

Grizzly paced the dark cell with his fists clenched at his sides, his suppressed anger close to the boiling point.

The room was ten feet by ten, its walls and door constructed of old wood. Devoid of all furniture, lacking even a sink, the cell reeked of sweat and urine. The floor was compact earth.

How long did the Vampires intend to keep him confined?

Grizzly paused and glanced at the door. He'd lost track of the hours spent in the cell, and he was growing increasingly impatient as the time passed. Six Vampires had dumped him in the cell last night, untied the ropes securing him to the pole, then departed with the pole and the ropes. By his estimation it was now the following afternoon, and not one Vampire had shown its ugly face all day. His stomach was growling and he needed to relieve himself, but he had a greater worry.

Where was Athena?

He walked to the cell door and peered out the narrow barred slot situated at eye level. An empty, dim corridor stretched before him. A single lantern was attached to a metal hook ten yards from the door, casting feeble light on the wooden walls and dirt floor. Some of the light filtered in the cell window, affording the only illumination.

Why didn't he just break out? he asked himself.

Grizzly frowned as he stared at the corridor. He knew the answer to that one: He wouldn't do anything to endanger Athena. If he escaped, the Vampires might kill her before he could find her. Locating Athena before he made his bid for freedom was imperative.

Then he would take care of the damn Vampires!

His keen ears detected the quiet padding of naked feet on the dirt floor of the corridor.

A pale figure appeared, heading toward the cell.

Grizzly watched until he recognized the approaching Vampire, then he backed into the darkest corner.

Seconds later a cruel, angular face materialized at the barred slot. "Grizzly?" Waxlike eyes shifted from right to left. "Ahhh! There you are? What are you trying to do? Hide?" the figure asked and tittered.

"To what do I owe this honor, Polidori?" Grizzly asked. He did not mention that standing in the corner had been a purposeful test of the Vampire's vision.

"Would you like some food?" Polidori inquired.

Grizzly moved to the door. "I get to eat?" he rejoined in surprise.

"Of course," Polidori stated. "We don't want you to become weak and sick."

"Why all this concern about my health?" Grizzly questioned.

"The healthier, the bettter," Polidori replied enigmatically. "I'm sure a bright mutant like you can figure it out, Grizzly."

On the verge of telling the Vampire where to shove its sarcasm, Grizzly tensed and placed his hands on the door. "You called me by my name!"

Polidori tittered. "Yep. Definitely a bright mutant!"

"I never told you my name," Grizzly stated. "How did you find out?"

"From your sweetheart," Polidori replied.

"My sweetheart?"

"Athena," Polidori said with a smirk. "I do admire your taste in women. She's a fox."

Grizzly's nostrils flared. "Where is she? What have you done to her?"

"We haven't done anything to her," Polidori said. "Yet. Corpus has given orders she's not to be touched."

"Who is Corpus?" Grizzly asked.

"The head of the Venesects, stupid," Polidori replied.

"If he lays a hand on her—" Grizzly began.

Polidori laughed. "Didn't you hear what I just said? Corpus has ordered us not to lay a finger on her. She's not to be used as foodstuff." He sighed. "Too bad. She's a healthy specimen."

"Why is Athena receiving special treatment?" Grizzly inquired.

"Because of you," Polidori responded.

"Me?"

"Yeah, dummy. You. Corpus has taken a personal interest in your case. And when I told him that you're hot to trot for the bitch, he decided to use her to keep you in line," Polidori detailed.

Grizzly could feel his temper rising. "I want to meet this Corpus."

"You will," Polidori promised.

"When?"

"Tonight. Corpus is holding a banquet in your honor." Polidori snickered. "And the bitch will be there too."

"What about the people you abducted from Aguanga?" Grizzly questioned.

"All of them will be at the banquet," Polidori said. "They'll be the highlight of the night."

"What do you mean?"

"You'll see," Polidori said, then snickered. "Now how about a snack to tide you over until the banquet?"

"I'm not hungry," Grizzly lied. "But I do need to use a bathroom."

Polidori cackled. "A bathroom! What do you think the corners of your cell are for?"

"If I go in here it'll stink up the whole room," Grizzly remarked.

"Poor baby!" Polidori mocked him.

"At least let me out to go somewhere else," Grizzly said.

"No way."

"I won't try to escape," Grizzly stated. "You have my

word.''

Polidori's eyes narrowed. "I don't trust you. But Corpus did say you wouldn't try a thing as long as we have the bitch.''

"So let me out,'' Grizzly prompted.

"Why should I do you any favors?'' Polidori asked. "What's in it for me?''

"Just my gratitude,'' Grizzly said.

Polidori started laughing. He laughed and laughed, doubling over, his hands pressed against his ribs.

"What's so funny?'' Grizzly demanded.

Polidori slowly straightened, his laughter trailing off. He took a deep breath. "You are!''

Grizzly did not respond.

"You're the funniest guy I've met in ages!'' Polidori declared. "Do you think I care about your gratitude?''

"Then let me out for another reason,'' Grizzly proposed.

"Like what?''

"When I get around to killing you, I won't make you suffer,'' Grizzly pledged. "But only if you let me out.''

Polidori began laughing again.

Grizzly frowned. He knew insanity when he saw it, and Polidori was definitely off the deep end. Perhaps all of the Vampires were tainted by hereditary mental instability.

"You're a regular comedian!'' Polidori stated. "And I'll tell you what I'll do. I'll let you out to take your dump, but I'm going to hold you to your promise. I wouldn't want to suffer!'' He burst into a hearty guffaw.

Grizzly waited for the Vampire's mirth to subside. He regretted making his hasty pledge. If anyone deserved to suffer, Polidori did.

"But remember,'' the Vampire said, suddenly serious. "Any funny stuff and the bitch buys the farm! They're expecting me back soon.''

"Who is?''

"Corpus, Loring, and Minshi,'' Polidori said. He reached out and slid a metal bolt from its socket, then retreated several paces. "Okay. Come out.''

Grizzly opened the door and stepped into the corridor. His cell was located at the end of the passage.

"Follow me," Polidori instructed. "I'll find you a place to potty."

They walked along the corridor.

"You've mentioned the name Loring twice," Grizzly noted. "Who is he?"

"Loring is second in command to Corpus," Polidori answered. "Loring was in charge of the foodstuff hunt we were on when we captured you. He was the first one who jumped you in the gorge."

"Didn't I break his nose?"

"No. That was Prest. He's pissed about it too. He wanted to finish you on the spot, but Loring stopped him," Polidori said.

"And who is Minshi?" Grizzly asked.

Polidori abruptly halted and glanced back at the mutant. "Minshi is in a class all by himself."

"How's that?" Grizzly queried.

"You'll see." He stepped past the lantern.

Grizzly wanted to learn more information while Polidori was in a talkative mood. "What's with the lantern? You certainly don't need the light to see by."

"True," Polidori said. "Venesects can see in near total darkness. But we keep one lantern in each corridor for the benefit of the foodstuff. They can't see shit in the dark."

"Do you mean the people the Vampires have kidnapped?"

"Of course, moron," Polidori replied.

"They have the run of this place?" Grizzly probed.

"Some do," Polidori responded. "We use them for menial labor. We spare them if they do good work."

"Have any tried to escape?" Grizzly asked.

"No one has ever escaped from the Heartland," Polidori boasted. "And no one ever will."

"Then I'll be the first," Grizzly commented.

Polidori cackled.

They reached another cell door on the right side of the passage.

"Let's try this one," Polidori suggested. He opened the door and peered inside. "This one isn't occupied. Dump in here."

Grizzly entered the cell, a virtual carbon copy of the original.

He crossed to the far right-hand corner, then noticed Polidori was watching him. "Out. I don't need an audience."

"Bashful, huh?" Polidori said. He closed the door.

"No peeking," Grizzly warned as he squatted.

"Are the others as weird as you?" Polidori inquired.

"What others?" Grizzly responded, grunting.

"Your friends. The four men you were with. An Indian, a soldier, another guy in buckskins, and a giant."

"I don't know who you're talking about," Grizzly said.

"Sure you don't!" Polidori retorted. "Maybe it will refresh your memory when you see them at the banquet."

"They're here!" Grizzly exclaimed.

"One of our lookouts spotted them earlier," Polidori revealed. "Corpus ordered them to be captured. You'd better hope my brothers get to them before something else does. There are a lot of mutants in the Heartland, infesting the upper levels."

Grizzly was alarmed at the news. Blade as walking into a trap! Should he try to warn the Warrior? How could he, when he had no idea where to find the Force? "Say," he said casually, "I've been meaning to ask you something. You blindfolded me before you carted me down here. How far are we below the surface?"

The Vampire did not answer.

"Polidori? Did you hear me? How far are we below the surface?" Grizzly repeated.

No reply.

Puzzled, Grizzly finished and stood. Where was a large leaf when he needed one? He walked to the door and attempted to open it.

The cell door was locked.

"Polidori? What is this?" Grizzly demanded. He pressed his nose to the barred slot.

Forty yards off the Vampire's pale figure was gradually receding.

"Polidori! You son of a bitch! You tricked me!" Grizzly shouted, incensed.

Polidori paused long enough to yell a sarcastic reply. "No shit!"

The Vampire's laughter filled the corridor.

# CHAPTER TWELVE

The monstrosity, as Thunder had indicated, was as big a horse. Blade trained the Commando on the creature as it gathered itself to attack.

Eight feet tall at the shoulder and six feet wide, a gargantuan beetle blocked their path. Its six sturdy legs supported an ovoid body covered by green, armorlike fore wings, and an elongated neck and head, both black. Extending an arm's length from the head were two formidable, serrated mandibles clicking together in anticipiation of its next meal.

Blade fired, the Commando thundering eerily, booming and reverberating from the lofty spires, slag, and girders. The wooden stock bucked against his right side as the heavy slugs tore into the beetle.

Chittering in anguish, the creature halted for a second. It lowered its head and charged, absorbing the hail of lead without apparent effect.

Sergeant Havoc, Boone and Thunder were momentarily unable to aid the Warrior; he stood between the beetle and them. Boone darted to the right, Thunder to the left, both intending to provide covering fire. But before either could squeeze off a shot the beetle was on the giant.

Blade, firing all the while, endeavored to leap to the left to avoid the creature's rush. He failed. The beetle swung its head, its right mandible slamming into Blade and sending him sprawling onto his stomach. Before he could rise, the creature pounced.

"Blade!" Boone shouted.

Blade rolled over just as the creature reached him. The Commando was on the ground to his right. Any thought of retrieving the machine gun was instantly curtailed as the beetle's mandibles speared for his neck. He instinctively reached up, catching the mandibles in his brawny hands, gripping them by the outer edges. His muscles bulged as he held them aloft.

A contest of strength ensued, the beetle slowly, inexorably lowering its mandibles closer and closer to its prey as the Warrior struggled to keep them at bay.

Thunder ran to the head of the mutant and pressed the barrel of his M-16 against the beetle's left compound eye, then fired a short burst.

The creature did not so much as flinch, and now its mandibles were within six inches of the Warrior's neck.

Blade's biceps and triceps seemed to be sculpted from steel. Perspiration beaded his forhead, and every vein on his crimson face was protruding.

Sergeant Havoc closed in, his M-16 in his left hand, a metallic object in his right. He swung the automatic rifle like a club, striking the beetle's foreleg.

The mutant wrenched loose from the Warrior's grip and swung toward the noncom.

Havoc frantically backpedaled. "Get away from it!" he yelled. "Get away from it!" He brandished the object in his right hand.

The grenade.

Thunder and Boone dove for the nearest cover.

Blade surged to his feet and sprinted for the jagged wall.

The beetle bore down on the noncom.

And Havoc, hobbling toward a mound of slag, yanked the pin and tossed the grenade overhand. He took a painful, flying leap and landed behind the slag.

Blade was a yard from the wall when the grenade exploded. The concussion felt like a sledgehammer blow to the back as he was picked up and flung into the wall. Agony lanced his ribs as he slumped to the dirt, his senses swirling. He gulped in air and pushed himself to his knees.

The beetle was history, its head, neck, and the front section of its body all gone, the rear portion lying in the dust. Gruesome, pulpy pieces were scattered everywhere.

Boone stepped from in back of a pile of debris. "That was too close for comfort!"

Thunder walked around a twisted girder. He scanned the heights. "There could be more."

"I hope not," Sergeant Havoc muttered, rising from behind the mound of slag. He glanced at the Warrior. "Hey! Are you okay?"

Blade nodded, then stood. He slowly approached the carcass, his gray eyes roving the ground for his Commando. His lips curled downward when he found it. The machine gun had been caught in the blast; the stock was shattered, the barrel split and twisted. "Damn!" he snapped.

The others joined him.

"You still have Grizzly's M-16," Boone offered by way of a condolence.

"I know," Blade said. "But I liked that gun."

Sergeant Havoc stared at the grisly remains of the beetle. "I can't wait to get out of this Dead Zone."

"You and me both," Boone concurred. He gazed at the noncom. "Why didn't you use that grenade on the worm?"

Havoc averted his eyes and mumbled a few words.

"What? I didn't catch that," Boone said.

"I completely forgot about it," Sergeant Havoc admitted sheepishly.

Thunder was scrutinizing the passageways. "We should not stay here. The explosion will attract the Vampires."

Blade unslung the M-16 from his left shoulder. "You're right. Havoc, if you have any problems keeping up, just sing out."

"You can count on it," Sergeant Havoc said.

Blade returned to the junction. The Vampire tracks took the left branch, which might indicate the Vampires would be coming from that direction. He did not want to run into the Vampires just yet. To succeed in the mission he needed to capture a

Vampire. He would pick the time and place. "We'll go straight," he stated, and did so.

The passage proceeded in a direct westerly line for several hundred yards, then curved to the south, winding deeper and deeper into the ruins. Odd noises sounded occasionally: twitters and flutters and barks and growls. Once something howled.

Blade slowed as the passage widened. A spacious circular area appeared, a hundred yards across and ringed by imposing, ravaged edifices. Shafts of sparkling sunlight filtered down. Chunks of concrete, bricks, melted metal, demolished vehicles, and other legacies to humankind's destructive propensities formed heaps of various sizes. A narrow path threaded among the piles.

The air overhead was unexpectedly rent by the flapping of large wings.

Blade looked up, but all he saw was the sunlight and the shadows.

"What was that?" Boone asked in a hushed tone.

"I didn't see it," Sergeant Havoc said.

Thunder, the last in line, was gazing rearward. "We are being followed," he announced quietly.

"How do you know?" Boone questioned.

"I know," Thunder asserted.

Blade knew the Flathead was right. He had sensed someone . . . or something . . . on their trail for the past fifteen minutes. "We'll take cover," he declared, and led them into the labyrinth of debris. Thirty yards further he found the perfect ambush site.

To the right of the path was an antique yellow bus resting on its rusted undercarriage. There was no trace of the tires, all of the windows were missing, and the door was ajar and crumpled outward. The yellow paint was peeling and faded, the body marred by countless cracks.

"There," Blade said. He walked to the door and peeked inside. Some of the seats were still bolted to the floor, the cushions long since deteriorated. Detached seat frames littered the floor.

"What's the plan?" Boone inquired.

"We'll wait in here," Blade stated. "If the Vampires are after us, then we'll spring a little surprise on them. I want one alive."

He stepped into the bus and moved to the center, the floor creaking and rattling underfoot. The side of the bus faced the path, affording an ideal field of fire. He crouched below one of the windows.

Sergeant Havoc, Boone, and Thunder positioned themselves, with Thunder nearest the door. They waited in expectant silence.

Blade wondered if he had bitten off more than he could chew. The Dead Zone was a particularly perilous realm, with lethal manaces seemingly lurking behind every corner. Four men might not be enough to accomplish the mission, not when there could be hundreds of Vampires to deal with, Vampires who knew the Zone well. The Vampires enjoyed a decided, possibly insurmountable, advantage.

A faint footfall terminated his reflection.

The Warrior elevated his head until he could see over the lower edge of the window.

Ten yards separated the bus from the path. Another 15 yards to the rear was the first in a line of Vampires, nine in all. They were in a hurry, the leader with his eyes glued to the path.

Blade waited. He wanted the Vampires alongside the bus before he sprang the trap.

The Vampire leading the pursuit halted abreast of the bus. He knelt and examined the tracks in the dust, then rose and pivoted toward the vehicle.

Blade could see the Vampire's glassy eyes widening in consternation. He raised the M-16 to his right shoulder, sighted, and fired, his initial rounds smacking into the lead Vampire's head and catapulting the ghoul backwards.

Sergeant Havoc, Boone, and Thunder took their cue from the Warrior. Each cut loose with skilled precision.

Caught in the open in a writhing spray of automatic gunfire, the Vampires were decimated. Six dropped in half as many seconds, their bodies riddled with holes. Two foolishly tried to reach the bus and were cut to ribbons. Only one was left alive, and he wheeled and attempted to flee.

Boone was quicker. The Cavalryman drew his right Hombre, his arm a streak, and fired from the hip.

The shot was unerringly on target, the slug tearing into the Vampire's left foot, penetrating his ankle. He shrieked as he went down.

Blade didn't bother with the door. He gripped the upper rim of the window, lifted his legs, and vaulted to the ground. In five bounds he reached the Vampire and shoved the M-16 into the man's face. "Freeze!" he commanded.

The Vampire wasn't going anywhere. He was on his right side, clutching his leg above his splintered ankle and grimacing in anguish. "Finish me, you bastard!" he snapped. "Finish me!" He glared up at the giant.

Blade was surprised to note that the Vampire's nose was disfigured, bent to the left and swollen. "Keep your mouth shut unless I say otherwise!"

The Vampire's eyes were simmering pools of hatred. "Or what? You don't scare me!"

Boone, Thunder, and Sergeant Havoc surrounded their prisoner.

"The rest are dead," Havoc confirmed.

"We don't scare you?" Boone asked the Vampire.

For an answer, the Vampire tilted his head and tried to spit on the Cavalryman's moccasins.

Boone was holding his M-16 in his left hand, the Hombre in his right. He suddenly swept his right arm down, ramming the Hombre barrel into the Vampire's left eye and cocking the revolver.

The Vampire stiffened.

"If I were you," Boone advised in a grating tone, "I'd be real scared. Because if you flap your gums again without permission, your bloodsucking days will be over. Savvy?"

"Ye . . . Ye . . . Yes!" the Vampire stuttered.

Sergeant Havoc looked at Boone and grinned in appreciation.

"Now," Blade stated, "I want some answers. For starters, what's your name?"

"Prest."

"Are there more of your kind after us?" Blade interrogated him.

"Not at the moment," Prest replied, then smirked. "But there will be! Soon! You don't stand a chance!"

Blade gestured at the nearby ruins. "Is this your home base?"

"This is the Heartland," Prest said.

"Why do you call it the Heartland?" Blade asked.

"It was named the Heartland before I was born," Prest responded. "No one ever told me the reason."

"How old are you?"

"Twenty-seven."

"And how many Vampires live here?" Blade questioned.

"I don't know the exact count," Prest said. "The last I heard, there were something like two hundred and eighty."

"That's all?" Blade said skeptically.

"It's more than enough to take care of you four," Prest commented. "You'll never leave the Heartland alive!"

"We'll see," Blade said. "We're searching for two friends of ours. One of them, a woman wearing fatigues, was captured by Vampires. We don't know—"

"Quit calling us Vampires!" Prest interrupted.

"What?"

"We don't like that name," Prest said. "We're Venesects, damn it!"

"You prefer to be called Venesects?" Blade asked.

"You outsiders call us Vampires. It's your word, not ours," Prest stated.

"Venesects it is then," Blade said. "Where will we find your fellow Venesects?"

Prest's eyes shifted nervously. "Here and there."

"Not good enough," Blade informed him. "The Venesects must occupy a certain area in the Heartland, a place you call home. Where is this place?"

"I'll never tell," Prest said defiantly.

Blade glanced at Boone.

The Cavalryman jabbed the Hombre barrel into the Vampire's left eye again. "I'll count to three," he warned.

"I'll never tell!" Prest reiterated.

"One," Boone began.

Prest licked his red lips.

"Two," Boone said.

"Never!" Prest shouted, his right eye twitching uncontrollably.

"Thr—" Boone said.

"All right! All right!" Prest cried. "I'll talk!"

Boone stared at the Vampire for a moment, then twirled the Hombre into its holster.

"Where will we find your home base?" Blade queried impatiently.

Prest glowered at the giant as he replied. "The lower levels to the south."

"You'll take us there," Blade ordered. "Before we head out, I want to know about our friends, a woman in fatigues and a mutant with the features of a bear."

"That son of a bitch!" Prest spat.

"You've seen him?"

Prest raised his left hand and pointed at his nose. "Who the hell do you think did this?"

"What about the woman?" Blade pressed him. "Have you seen her too?"

"Yeah," Prest admitted.

"Are they alive?" Blade inquired, leaning forward.

"The last I knew," Prest said.

Blade straightened and studied their prisoner. The Vampires, or Venesects, were not fear-inspiring in the daylight. Prest was a prime example; he was more revolting than fierce. His pale skin, crimson lips, and glassy eyes lent him a sickly aspect. His thin frame appeared to be malnourished. Prest wasn't a mutant, but he wasn't entirely human.

"What are you staring at?" Prest snapped.

"Can you walk?" Blade asked.

Prest lifted his left leg. Watery, pinkish blood covered his foot, ankle, and shin. "What do you think, asshole?"

Blade glanced at Thunder. "Find something he can use as a crutch."

"Right away," Thunder said and moved off.

Blade stared upward at the shafts of sunlight. Nightfall would descend in a few hours, and the night was the Vampires' element. He did not relish the prospect of being in the Heartland after dark. In addition to the Vampires there were other dangers to worry about, creepy-crawly things with a craving for flesh. Vile things, unleashed by the transmutative capacity of radiation. Things an unsuspecting prewar world would never have envisioned.

"How about this?" Thunder said, intruding on the Warrior's musing. He held a shoulder-high length of rusty pipe.

"Do you expect me to use that?" Prest demanded.

"You'll use it," Boone stated, "or I'll plug you in the other foot and you can crawl all the way."

Prest's thin lips curled back from his tapered teeth. "You're mine! When the time comes, you're mine!"

"On your feet," Blade ordered.

The Vampire took the proffered pipe, then used it as a brace under his left arm so he could shuffle to a standing position. He dangled his left foot above the ground, his pink blood spattering the dust underneath.

"Move out," Blade directed.

Prest took a tentative step with the makeshift crutch.

"How far must we travel?" Blade inquired.

"Four miles or so," Prest replied.

Sergeant Havoc glanced at Blade. "At the rate he can move with the crutch," he commented, "we'll take all night."

"We'll do the best we can," Blade said. He prodded the Vampire with his M-16. "And if I get the impression you're stalling, I'll let Boone have you."

Prest gazed at the Cavalryman. "Is that your name? Boone?" Boone nodded.

Prest smiled malevolently. "I'll carve it on your forehead before I'm done with you."

Boone caught a whiff of the Vampire's breath and scrunched up his nose. "Whew! What did you do? Eat a skunk today?"

If looks could kill, Prest would have slain the Cavalryman on the spot.

Sergeant Havoc nudged Boone with his right elbow. "It's easy to understand why these clowns have bad breath."

"It is?" Boone responded.

"Sure. They're full of it up to here," Havoc said, then touched his nose.

# CHAPTER THIRTEEN

**P**olidori halted in front of a pair of huge wooden doors. He turned and grinned at the captive. "Are you ready?"

"Quit playing games and open the damn door!" Grizzly snapped.

One of the four Vampires behind the mutant, one of the quartet assigned to serve as his escort to the banquet, snickered. "He doesn't have much of a sense of humor, does he?"

"No," Polidori mentioned. "It's pitiful." He made a show of sniffing the musty air. "At least he had the decency to put on some cologne."

The quartet laughed.

Polidori faced the doors, gripped the metal knob on the door on the right, then shoved.

Grizzly, expecting a dilapidated banquet filled with slovenly Vampires, was genuinely astounded. He walked through the doorway, surveying the impressive setup.

"Not bad, huh?" Polidori said with evident pride.

"Not bad," Grizzly mumbled.

The banquet hall was enormous, 100 yards wide and 50 yards from the front doors to the rear wall. A vaulted ceiling arched above a white, tiled floor. Eight radiant chandeliers, brimming with candles instead of light bulbs, were suspended from the ceiling at twelve foot intervals the width of the chamber. Large wooden tables, aligned edge to edge, had been arranged in a horseshoe shape with the open end toward the front doors. Hundreds of Vampires and dozens of humans were milling about the hall, males and females.

"Corpus had this built," Polidori said to Grizzly. "Most of the material came from the towns and settlements we've raided."

A bell suddenly pealed, the notes vibrant and clangorous.

The Vampires and humans immediately took seats at the tables, the humans pulling out the wooden chairs so the Vampires could sit down. Then the humans seated themselves.

Grizzly stared at a veritable sea of pale countenances and sinister eyes, and for a second his confidence wavered. An uneasy sensation developed in the pit of his stomach.

A tall Vampire at the head of the horseshoe was the only one standing. He beckoned with his right arm. "Come in, Grizzly. We have been expecting you."

Polidori prodded the bear-man by slapping his left shoulder. "Get a move on! Don't keep Corpus waiting."

Grizzly walked toward the tall Vampire. He ignored the hungry gazes fixed on him by the Vampires, but he could feel his skin prickling just the same, especially under the fur at the nape of his neck.

"Welcome," the tall Vampire said. "You are our guest of honor tonight." A large golden bell on a metal tripod was visible to his rear.

Grizzly appraised the tall Vampire as he approached the table from the opposite side. This Vampire was different from the rest. Grizzly could see the difference in his handsome, regal facial lines, in the square thrust of his shoulders, in his alert green eyes. He wore a brown loincloth that was immaculate. While not exceptionally muscular, he was superbly proportioned. His long hair, unlike the dark hair of the majority of the Vampires, was white. Grizzly stopped behind a chair directly across from this unique Vampire. He nodded once. "So you're the head scumbag."

Abrupt intakes of breath punctuated the assembled Vampires and humans.

"There is no need to be insulting," the tall Vampire said. "And yes, I am Corpus."

"You're awful polite for a rotten Vampire," Grizzly commented.

Corpus's eyes bored into the mutant. "Why are you deliberately baiting me? I invited you here as my personal guest. No harm has befallen you." He paused. "And please don't refer to us as Vampires. We are Venesects."

"Vampires are bloodsucking leeches," Grizzly said. "If the shoe fits . . ." He let the sentence trail off.

Corpus sighed. "If you persist in this crude behavior, I will be compelled to have you returned to your cell. Which is unfortunate, because I was under the impression you wanted to see Ms. Morris again."

Grizzly tensed. "Athena is here?"

"She will be, shortly," Corpus replied. "Now what will it be? Will you behave in a civilized fashion, or do you want to languish in a miserable cell? The choice is yours."

Grizzly pulled out the chair and sat down. "So what's on the menu?" He noticed four brown leather straps affixed to the table top.

Corpus smiled and slowly seated himself. "A special meal is being prepared for you. I'd like to surprise you."

A thin Vampire with a hook nose and a cleft chin, in the chair to Corpus's right, placed his elbows on the table and folded his hands. "Can you imagine the vitality?" he asked.

"Vitality?" Grizzly repeated quizzically.

"A superb specimen," Corpus said to the hooked-nosed Vampire. "Grizzly, I would like you to meet Loring. He's my right-hand man."

"I've heard about him," Grizzly mentioned.

"Oh?" Loring said.

"From Polidori," Grizzly disclosed. He looked around for the tittering Vampire, but Polidori was gone. A female Vampire ten feet to the right drew his attention. He realized that all the female Vampires covered their breasts with strips of pliable brown leather.

"Have you also heard about my brother, Minshi?" Corpus inquired, nodding at the doors.

Grizzly shifted in his seat, his eyes widening slightly.

A colossal Vampire was coming into the banquet hall. In size and build he strongly resembled Blade. His face, though, was a mask of latent cruelty. Huge hands swung at his sides. His skin tone was extraordinarily white, his eyes pinpoints of feral luminosity. A black loincloth encircled his waist.

"He's your brother?" Grizzly said.

"My younger brother," Corpus responded. "I have the brains, he supplies the brawn. He is most devoted and serves as my official executioner. There were a few Venesects who opposed my plans. Believe it or not, under Minshi's influence all dissension has been eradicated."

"I believe it," Grizzly assured the Vampire leader.

Minshi was within ten feet of the head table when he moved to one side, revealing the woman following him. His immense form had obscured her until that moment.

"Athena!" Grizzly exclaimed, rising.

Athena took one look and raced up to him. She flung her arms around his neck and hugged him tightly. "Grizzly! I didn't think I'd ever see you again!"

Grizzly felt a peculiar constriction in his throat. He coughed and held her at arm's length. "I'm here to rescue you. Have any of them touched you?"

Athena shook her head. "They put me in a small room with just a cot. Polidori visited me once. No one else showed up until a few minutes ago." She glanced at Minshi and shuddered.

"Please have a seat," Corpus stated courteously, standing. "I have looked forward to meeting you. I am Corpus."

Athena studied the Vampire. "Polidori told me about you."

"And me about you," Corpus said. "Have a seat." He pointed at an empty chair to Grizzly's right.

Athena complied, her eyes narrowing as she beheld the leather straps.

Grizzly sat back down, overwhelmed with relief at discovering Athena was unharmed.

Minshi walked up to the table on Grizzly's left.

"Go check on Polidori," Corpus instructed his brother. "We don't want to delay the festivities."

"As you wish," Minshi said gruffly. He spun and departed.

Corpus gazed at Grizzly and Athena. "Would either of you care for some wine before the main course? We have an excellent selection of white and red wines."

Grizzly and Athena exchanged surprised expressions.

"You drink wine?" Grizzly commented in disbelief.

"No," Corpus answered. "But many on our human staff do. Our dietary requirements are quite different."

"I know," Grizzly said. "You specialize in drinking blood."

"Do you hold our nutritional needs against us?" Corpus asked.

"Nutritional needs!" Grizzly declared, then snorted. "There's a good one! Killing innocent people in cold blood isn't my idea of obtaining proper nutrition."

"When I say nutritional needs, I mean precisely that," Corpus stated defensively. He gazed from the bear-man to the woman. "Perhaps an explanation is called for. Are you familiar with the origin of the Venesects?"

"They crawled out from a slimy rock," Grizzy quipped.

"Be nice," Corpus said sternly.

Athena surveyed the banquet hall and the crowded tables. "How did all of this come about?"

"I will gladly provide the details," Corpus offered. "But first, would either of you like some wine? I'm afraid it's the only liquid refreshment we possess for human consumption. We do not bother with storing water because we don't drink it."

"I would," Athena said. "I'd like a glass of white wine."

"And you?" Corpus asked Grizzly.

"No thanks."

Corpus shrugged. "Suit yourself." His right hand disappeared below the table and produced a small golden hammer. "This bell was appropriated from a Spanish-style church near the border," he divulged, twisting in his seat. He reached out and tapped the bell lightly twice.

A door in the rear wall, ten feet to the right, instantly opened. A man appeared, a human dressed in a white shirt, white pants, and an apron. He hurried over to Corpus. "You rang, sir?"

"A goblet of our best white wine for the lady," Corpus directed.

"Certainly, sir." The man in white wheeled and hastened to obey.

Grizzly shook his head in disgust. "Did you house-train him yourself?"

Corpus eyed the mutant for several seconds. "Why should you care for these humans? What are they to you? I am not ignorant, you know. I'm aware of current developments in the world. Most humans dislike mutants, so why should you care for them?"

"I wouldn't say I care for them very much," Grizzly replied. "But I don't like seeing others made into slaves, whether they're humans, mutants, or otherwise."

Athena could sense a friction between the two. Her happiness at being reunited with Grizzly after so many hours of anxiety and terror was tempered by her perception of their predicament. "You mentioned an explanation," she said, hoping to defuse a confrontation.

Corpus leaned back in his chair and surveyed the hall. "We have come a long way since the war, and greater glories are on our horizon."

"The Vampires . . ." Athena began, and then remembered the name Polidori had used during their earlier discussion. "I'm sorry. The Venesects arose after the war?"

"Yes," Corpus confirmed. "We possess the written records of our ancestors. They relate a fascinating tale." He stared absently at the ceiling. "Millions of people were living in San Diego when the nuclear missile hit. Apparently they received twenty minute's advance warning from the authorities. Most attempted to flee. Some resigned themselves to their fate. And a few retired to special shelters, fallout shelters, hoping to survive the nuclear explosion."

The man in white returned bearing a crystal goblet containing white wine. He reached across the table and deposited the goblet near Athena.

"Thank you," she said.

He nodded and left.

"As I was saying," Corpus continued. "A few San Diego residents huddled in below-ground fallout shelters—trembling in fear, no doubt. One of these shelters, located in the southern section of the city, was constructed by a wealthy financier. This particular shelter was one hundred and fifty feet underground and could only be reached by a generator-powered elevator. Thirty-two people were in this shelter when the blast occurred.''

"They survived," Athena deduced.

"That they did," Corpus said. "Only to find themselves buried under tons of debris. The surface was too radioactive for them to venture above ground. They were forced to live like rats under the ruins, building tunnels where necessary, and foraging as best they could. Their stockpiled food eventually was exhausted. They tried subsisting on rodents, insects, and earthworms without success." He looked at Athena and Grizzly and smiled. "And then one of them had an inspiration."

"What kind of inspiration?" Athena queried.

"Using their own bodies as sustenance," Corpus responded.

Athena appeared horrified. "They became cannibalistic?"

Corpus laughed. "No. Nothing so extreme. They wanted to survive, not destroy themselves. One of them, a physician, hit on a novel idea." He stared at Athena. "Liquid nourishment or solid food? Which is more essential to human survival?"

"A person can survive longer without food than without water or another liquid," Athena answered. "The human body is three-fourths water. I read somewhere that the average person can live for up to two months without food and not suffer any irreparable harm. But we can't go much more than a week without water."

"Exactly," Corpus concurred. "So for the survivors, their primary concern was discovering a source of liquid nourishment. And what better source than their own blood?"

Athena's lips curled downward distastefully. "Their blood?"

"What else?" Corpus rejoined. "Blood is exceptionally rich in vitamins and minerals. Take iron as an example. Humans need iron. Four tablespoons of blood can supply the typical adult's daily iron requirement. Blood also contains proteins and sugar. As a source of nourishment for the survivors, blood was ideal. Even more crucial was the fact that blood is constantly being manufactured by the body. Blood is renewable. A healthy person can give a pint of blood every six to eight weeks with no ill effects."

"So your ancestors took to drinking their blood to stay alive," Grizzly remarked in fascination.

Corpus nodded. "Their blood, supplemented by whatever other liquid foodstuffs they could find. The Venesects have existed on this diet for over a century."

Athena gazed at the Vampires to her right and left. "I think I'm beginning to understand. Your ancestors were compelled to live underground for decades because of the excessive radiation. By the time your people could venture safely above the surface, their bodies had adjusted to a subterranean life-style. Their eyes had adapted to the limited light below ground, which meant they couldn't venture abroad in the daylight because the bright sun would damage their vision."

"Excellent," Corpus said. "Most perceptive."

"This explains the reason you conduct your raids at night," Athena went on. "Why you travel at night and rest during the day, avoiding the sunlight as much as possible."

"Any other insights?" Corpus encouraged her.

"Yes," Athena said. "Your pale skin is caused by two factors. One, obviously, is the prolonged period the Venesects have lived underground. The second must be tied to a form of anemia. I'm not a doctor, but I've seen anemic patients at a hopsital. And some of your people are suffering the same symptoms."

"I am impressed," Corpus complimented her. "You have summarized our problem concisely. About thirty years after the war, our ancestors noticed a marked decline in their health and general vitality. They realized that they could not subsist on their own blood any longer. Their blood had become impoverished through a lack of certain vitamins and minerals. In order to restore their vitality they needed a fresh supply of vitamin-rich blood, a new source of nutrition. They started hunting for foodstuff on the surface at night."

"They started abducting people and bringing the victims down here to feed on," Grizzly interjected testily.

"Rudely put, but accurate," Corpus said. "What choice did we have? Either we acquired a new nutritional supply or we perished."

"Why didn't the Venesects try to live above ground again?" Athena inquired. "Why didn't your people try to wean themselves from their dependence on blood?"

"We did try," Corpus stated with a frown. "We were not successful. Our physiological evolution has acclimatized us irredeemably to our current status." He sighed. "There is no going back. We are what we have become and we will never be as we were."

"You can't go on like this," Athena commented. "Sooner or later the people on the surface will send in a military force and wipe you out."

"We took care of the last force sent against us," Corpus disclosed.

"That was just a platoon," Athena noted. "What happens if an army is sent?"

"We will cross that bridge when we come to it," Corpus philosophized. He looked up in the direction of the front doors, a wide grin creasing his features. "Ahhhh. They have arrived."

Grizzly turned in his chair.

Minshi, Polidori, and over a dozen other Vampires were escorting several dozen bedraggled, fatigued humans into the banquet hall. A ripple of excitement animated the Vampires seated at the tables; they began conversing in hushed tones, smiling in anticipation, and a few even licked their lips.

Corpus shifted and struck the golden bell hard three times.

All talking ceased. Every eye in the hall focused on the head Vampire.

"All human attendants will return to their quarters," Corpus commanded.

There was a commotion as five dozen humans rose and left the chamber, circling around the incoming captives.

"We don't permit the help to view our feasts," Corpus said to Grizzly. "Many Venesects have taken humans as mates or as personal servants. We wouldn't want to unduly upset them."

"Personal servants! Don't you mean personal slaves?" Grizzly queried.

"I'm beginning to believe you're a hopeless case," Corpus stated.

Minshi, Polidori, and their crew of Vampires had herded the frightened humans they were escorting into the open space between the arms of the horseshoe.

Two Vampires closed and bolted the huge doors.

"So we won't be disturbed," Corpus remarked.

"Who are these people?" Athena asked, staring at the 37 prisoners.

"They are from Aguanga," Corpus replied.

Athena tensed and glanced at the Vampire leader. "What do you intend to do with them?"

Corpus chuckled. "Please don't act naive."

Athena blanched and stood. "I want to leave."

Corpus's eyes narrowed. "Sit down," he instructed her harshly. "You've displayed an intense curiosity about us. What kind of host would I be if I did not satisfy your curiosity to its utmost?" He surveyed the assemblage. "Let the feeding commence!"

# CHAPTER FOURTEEN

"I think this turkey is stalling, sir," Sergeant Havoc mentioned.

"I am not!" Prest snapped. "I'd like to see you do any better on one foot."

Blade paused and scanned the corridor ahead. Closed doors lined both sides of the hall. A solitary lantern with a flickering flame cast ominous shadows on the walls.

"I've done what you wanted," Prest groused. "I'm sticking to the corridors we use the least. These rooms are for storage, mainly. You won't find many Venesects in this area."

"How soon will we reach our friends?" Blade asked.

"Soon," Prest assured the Warrior. "They're being held in cells on one of the lower levels."

Boone, who was fourth in line after the Vampire, Blade, and Sergeant Havoc, stared at the ceiling. "We keep going farther and farther underground. I don't trust this guy. He could be leading us into a trap."

"If he does," Blade said, "he'll be the first to die."

"I'm not stupid," Prest declared.

"That's debatable," Sergeant Havoc quipped.

"Up yours!" Prest retorted.

"Keep moving," Blade instructed the Vampire, then nudged him with the M-16 barrel.

"I'm doing the best I can!" Prest complained. He hobbled on the makeshift crutch toward the lantern.

Blade followed, glancing over his right shoulder at his men. Thunder was covering the rear. Boone was tensed, coiled for action. Sergeant Havoc seemed to be taking the strain in stride, and he was walking with a less pronounced limp. So far, so good. But how long would their luck hold? The Vampires were bound to discover their presence.

Unbeknownst to the Warrior, the Vampires already had.

Prest passed the lantern and proceeded to a junction. He took the left fork.

"This place is a maze," Blade commented. "And all the passageways look alike. How do you keep from getting lost?"

"We're born and raised down here," Prest said. "By the time I was ten I knew every tunnel, every corridor by heart. It's impossible for a Venesect to become lost," he boasted.

"Even on the surface?" Blade asked.

"The surface is a different story," Prest stated. "But we've traveled at night for decades. We can read the stars as well as anybody."

"How many guards will be posted at the cells?" Blade questioned.

"That depends on how many prisoners are being held," Prest replied.

In 50 yards they came to another junction.

"We go straight," Prest announced.

Blade noticed the dirt floor was gradually inclining downwards. Fewer and fewer doors appeared. A cool draft blew across his face. Where was the air coming from? Had the Vampires excavated ventilation shafts? He was about to pose the question to Prest when an astonishing thing happened: The Vampire abruptly soared like a bird.

Or seemed to.

One moment Prest was walking down the incline, his head and shoulders partially obscured by the murky blackness. The next he was flying through the air with his arms outstretched.

Blade automatically raised the M-16 and sighted on the aerial Vampire, but before he could squeeze the trigger another amazing happening prevented him from firing.

The floor dropped from under him.

The Warrior felt the dirt start to slide as the entire floor suddenly tilted at a sharp angle, then swiveled inward.

"What the—!" Sergeant Havoc exclaimed.

All four Force members pitched into the abyss below. Boone and Thunder endeavored to grab hold of the wall, their efforts frustrated by the smooth, slippery wood.

Blade realized an entire section of floor served as a gigantic trapdoor, and he envisioned being impaled on rows of pointed stakes or falling into a nest of ravenous mutants. Instead his boots made contact with a brittle, yet oddly resilient surface. Something crunched under his heels as he sank in to his knees. He nearly toppled forward but regained his balance. A putrid stench engulfed him.

Sergeant Havoc, Boone, and Thunder landed near the Warrior, their collective impact creating a racket of snapping, crackling, and popping noises.

Blade looked up. Dimly visible 25 feet overhead were the pale features of the Vampire. Prest's face was stationary, and Blade guessed that the Vampire was standing at the rim of the hole.

Prest uttered a triumphant laugh. "The tables have turned, you bastards!"

"Do you want me to pick him off, sir?" Sergeant Havoc whispered to Blade.

"Not yet," Blade said quietly, then raised his voice to address the Vampire. "That was a slick move, Prest."

"Damn straight it was!" Prest replied.

"How'd you do it?" Blade casually inquired, hoping to derive a clue as to the nature of the hole they were in.

"It was easy!" Prest gloated. "We set you up, chumps!"

"We?" Blade repeated.

Three more Vampires suddenly materialized alongside Prest.

"Where did they come from?" Blade asked.

"They were shadowing us for the past ten minutes," Prest answered. "I led you past one of the few guard posts we have on the lower levels. They hid until we were out of sight, then took a shortcut to reach the pit first.'' He snickered. ''They took care of unlatching the door.''

''The corridor was booby-trapped,'' Blade speculated.

''No, you idiot,'' Prest declared. ''This is our garbage pit.''

''Your garbage pit?'' Blade reiterated in surprise.

''That's right,'' Prest said. ''Let me explain. Decades ago we had a problem with our garbage. All the refuse was dumped in a big hole on one of the upper levels, and the dump became a breeding ground for mutants of all kinds. Bugs. Worms. You name it. They were drawn to the dump like vultures to carrion.'' He paused. ''We decided to do something about it. First we dug this new pit on the very lowest level, as far from most of the mutants as we could get. This corridor is a dead end. One way in, one way out. By posting guards farther up, we can prevent stray bugs from locating it. We even covered the pit with a swinging door to reduce the stench. Sometimes a worm will burrow into the pit, but we've pretty much eliminated the problem.''

''So the guards rigged the garbage-pit door to open when we were on it,'' Blade commented. ''And they covered it with dirt to hide it.''

''You've got it,'' Prest said, smirking.

''But how did you avoid falling in?'' Blade questioned. ''I didn't know Vampires could fly.''

The Vampires laughed.

''We can't,'' Prest stated. He made a motion with his right hand, as if he was tugging on something. ''There's a rope here. It's attached to a beam near the ceiling. We use it to lower down a lantern from time to time to inspect the pit for worms or other mutants. All I did was leap for the rope and swing across the pit while you jackasses were falling in. The guards extinguished the lantern we usually keep next to the pit door. It was too dark for you to see the rope, but I could see it clearly.'' He paused. ''And now you're our prisoners.''

''What do you intend to do with us?'' Blade inquired, then quickly whispered to Sergeant Havoc. ''Can you nail all four with one burst?''

''No problem,'' Havoc responded. ''Just say the word, sir.''

Prest seemed to lean forward. "What's going on down there?"

Blade had forgotten about the Vampire's keen eyesight and hearing. "We're just concerned about your intentions," he replied.

One of the Vampires abruptly disappeared.

"You can cool your heels down there while I go report to Corpus," Prest said. "Our leader will be very pleased."

"I can get those three, sir," Sergeant Havoc remarked in a barely audible tone.

"Not yet," Blade responded. Where was the fourth Vampire? He needed all four on the rim. If just one escaped, the alarm would be sounded and the Vampires would be after the Force en masse. He was relying on Havoc's skill with the M-16 to resolve the dilemma. Boone and Thunder were both expert marksmen. Thunder, in particular, was outstanding with a rifle. But Sergeant Havoc had used M-16's extensively and was the best shot in the California military.

"Keep an eye out for worms," Prest taunted them. "We wouldn't want anything to happen to you!"

A glow of light appeared above the garbage pit, and a second later the fourth Vampire stepped into view holding a lantern.

"Now?" Havoc whispered.

"Wait," Blade directed.

The fourth Vampire turned and attached the lantern to a metal loop imbedded in the wall at shoulder height.

"Get ready," Blade instructed softly.

Prest held his crutch aloft. "I won't be needing this any more. I put another one over on you! I could have walked at my normal speed! My ankle only hurt for a little while. We Venesects are more resistant to pain than you humans. Even serious injuries hardly faze us for long. We're practically impervious to harm," he boasted.

"You're not impervious to death," Blade remarked.

"So?" Prest rejoined.

"So die," Blade said, then shouted to Sergeant Havoc. "Now!"

Sergeant Havoc was cradling the M-16 with the stock pressed against his right hip and the barrel angled upwards. He simply shifted the barrel a few inches and squeezed the trigger.

The lantern light bathed the Vampires in a yellowish-orange radiance, clearly revealing their stupefied expressions as they were struck. The burst stitched their heads from right to left. Prest took the first slugs in the forehead, his mouth drooping, his body starting to slump over. The other three died in a spray of brains, hair, and flesh. Two of them fell backwards. One sprawled to the right. Prest plunged headfirst into the garbage pit.

Blade saw the Vampire's falling form dropping toward him and waded to the right, forcing his way through the reeking refuse.

The corpse slammed into the muck at the spot the Warrior vacated.

"Nice shooting," Blade complimented the noncom.

"They were overconfident," Havoc observed. "They shouldn't have exposed themselves."

For the first time since dropping into the pit, Blade surveyed his surroundings. The garbage pit was ten yards in circumference with sides of red earth. A disgusting stew of bones, excrement, and other sickening waste matter filled the pit to his knees. The lantern light accented every nauseating detail.

Boone was also scrutinizing the pit. "Yuck! Let's get out of here."

Blade gazed at the rim, pondering a plan. He could see the thick rope suspended from the beam, but the lower portion was out of sight. Was the bottom of the rope coiled on the corridor floor? Prest had mentioned using the rope to lower the lantern into the pit, so there must be additional footage. If one of them could reach that rope, escaping the pit would be an easy task.

But how to reach the rope?

"Look at all these bones!" Boone commented. "They look human."

"They are," Thunder said.

Blade spied the way out. The large trapdoor had swung inward and was now flush with one side of the pit, with the lower edge of the door 16 feet above his head. Close to the bottom edge, at the corners, were two metal rings. Normally, he reasoned, ropes were tied to the rings and strung over the beam to suspend the door over the pit. The Vampires must have removed the ropes so the door would drop when sufficient pressure was applied. He peered at the opposite rim, realizing the pit was wider at the bottom than the top by a good seven yards.

"How will we get out of here?" Boone asked.

Blade moved to the side and positioned himself directly under the trap door. "Thunder, come here."

The Flathead stepped over to the Warrior. "Yes?"

"I want you to climb onto my shoulders," Blade directed. "When you're ready, I'll give you a heave. You should be able to grab the bottom of the door. Take hold of one of the rings."

Thunder slung his M-16 over his shoulder. "How will I get from the ring to the top of the pit? There are no handholds on the door."

"Take my Bowies," Blade suggested. "Stick them in the door and use them to climb on."

"You should go," Thunder said. "You are much stronger than I."

"Could you bear my weight on your shoulders?" Blade inquired.

"Two of us could," Boone interjected, joining them. "Put one leg on my shoulder and one on his. We should be able to support you."

Blade pursed his lips in thought. They were right. He stood a better chance of reaching the rim. "Okay. Take this," he said, extending his M-16 toward Sergeant Havoc.

The noncom took the weapon.

Boone and Thunder situated themselves with their backs against the dirt side. The Cavalryman slung his M-16 over his right shoulder and cupped his hands. "Ready when you are."

Thunder cupped his hands and nodded.

Blade stared at the trap door, gauging the distance. He rubbed his hands together. "On the count of three."

"How much do you weigh, by the way?" Boone asked.

"About two hundred and sixty pounds," Blade replied.

Boone grinned. "Sorry I asked."

"One," Blade said, beginning the count. He would need to move as rapidly as possible, especially once he reached the door. His own weight would be a detriment. "Two."

"Good luck," Sergeant Havoc commented.

Boone and Thunder braced their legs.

"Three," Blade said. He placed his right boot in Thunder's hands, his left in Boone's, and quickly clambered onto their shoulders. His nose was nearly touching the earthern wall. Craning his neck, he gazed at the lower edge of the door four feet above his head.

"Hurry!" Boone prompted through clenched teeth. "You feel like you weigh a ton!"

Blade eased his right Bowie from its sheath, tensed his legs, and leaped, his left arm outstretched and grasping for the metal ring in the lower left corner. His fingers closed on the ring, providing the fleetest of purchases, but he was already in motion with his right arm, surging the Bowie up and in. The blade thudded into the wood, penetrating deeply, and held fast.

"You did it!" Boone cried, elated.

The Warrior sagged for a second, girding his strength, his arms rippling, his body flush with the side of the pit. The strain on his shoulders was tremendous! Concentrate! he told himself. Concentrate! The tricky part was next. He released the metal ring, his left hand flashing to his left Bowie and drawing the knife as he started to slump, his right arm laboring to support his entire weight. He drove the left Bowie overhand as far as he could reach, using his right arm to lift himself higher so that the left Bowie sank into the door three feet above the right one. He lifted his left leg and rested his foot on the metal ring.

He couldn't stop now!

Blade grunted as he looked up at the rim.

Six feet to go!

He tugged on the right Bowie, working the blade back and forth until the knife came free. His shoulder muscles bunching into knotted cords, he lunged upward yet again and imbedded the right Bowie in the door.

Dear Spirit! How his shoulders hurt!

Blade ignored the agony and focused on wrenching the left Bowie from the wood. His nostrils inhaled the dank, musty scent of the dirt wall. The left Bowie pulled free, and once more he raised the knife as high as he could and rammed the blade into the wood.

"You're almost there!" Boone yelled.

Breathing heavily, Blade tugged on the right Bowie until it came loose. He propelled himself higher and slammed the knife home, then glanced upward.

The rim was mere inches above his right hand!

He released the left Bowie and clutched the edge of the pit. With a monumental effort he propped his left forearm on the rim. Using his left arm for leverage, he let go of the right Bowie and braced his right forearm on top. Climbing all the way out was accomplished with relative ease, and he perched on the rim, squatting while he caught his breath.

"Don't forget us," Boone quipped.

Blade glanced down at the trapdoor. He would retrieve the Bowies after rescuing his companions.

"The rope!" Boone urged.

The Warrior grinned at the Cavalryman's eagerness to vacate the foul pit.

"Sometime this year!" Boone cracked.

Blade shifted toward the rope. As he'd expected, enough rope was coiled on the corridor floor to reach the bottom of the garbage hole. He rose and walked to the coils, then deftly tossed the rope over the side.

"Thanks," Boone called out.

Blade inspected each of the Vampires to insure they were dead. As he was examining the last one, inquisitively studying its pallid complexion, Boone appeared. The Cavalryman was climbing hand-over-hand up the rope.

"I thought I would be sick," Boone mentioned as he scaled the rim and straightened. "I couldn't wait to get out of there!" He looked down. "I'm up! Who's next?"

Blade walked to the edge.

Thunder was nimbly ascending.

The Warrior turned and gazed along the corridor. "Boone, I want you to go back to the nearest junction. Other Vampires may have heard Havoc's shots. If any show up, get here on the double."

Boone nodded and hastened off.

So what was their next move? Blade asked himself as he watched Thunder mount the rope. Prest had claimed that Athena and Grizzly were both in cells on one of the lower levels, but the Vampire was probably lying. Which meant the two could be anywhere.

The rope shook and swayed slightly as Thunder neared the top. He hoisted his body above the edge, then stepped to solid ground. "I'm up!" he shouted to Havoc.

Blade knelt and began scooping the dirt aside.

"What are you doing?" Thunder questioned.

"What is the trapdoor attached to?" Blade asked.

"I don't know," Thunder responded.

"Neither do I," Blade said. The trapdoor protruded from under the dirt, and six large metal hinges were visible, spaced at intervals on the inner edge. He scraped off the dirt behind one of the hinges and discovered the inner half of the hinge was riveted to a metal plate partially imbedded in a wide concrete foundation. Frustrated, he stood and sighed.

"Is something wrong?" Thunder inquired.

"I was thinking of rigging a booby trap for the Vampires to give them a taste of their own medicine," Blade explained. "But dismantling some of these hinges would take too much time."

Sergeant Havoc came up over the lip of the pit, an M-16 on each shoulder. He swung to the corridor floor and landed unsteadily, his left leg almost buckling. Grimacing, he caught himself and straightened.

"Your leg?" Blade said.

Havoc nodded. "It's worse than before. I twisted my left ankle when I fell into the pit."

"Can you walk?" Blade asked.

"I can manage," Havoc asserted.

Blade took a stride and grabbed the rope. "My Bowies are still in the door," he commented, then slid down until he was next to the top Bowie. He jerked the knife out and replaced it in his right sheath. A few seconds later he recovered the other Bowie, then climbed from the pit.

"Here's your M-16, sir," Havoc said, offering the automatic rifle.

Blade was reaching for the weapon when the shots sounded from the direction of the junction.

Boone!

# CHAPTER FIFTEEN

Athena Morris was shocked to the depths of her soul, horrified beyond measure. She saw the Vampires swarm upon the hapless captives from Aguanga. She heard the women and men scream as they were grasped securely, with five or six Vampires to each prisoner, and carted to the tables. Only then did she comprehend the significance of the leather straps attached to the tops of the tables.

Corpus was watching with a demented gleam to his eyes and a flush to his cheeks. Drool formed on his lips.

Polidori, Minshi, and three more Vampires were approaching the head table. They effortlessly carried a young woman between them. Terror contorted her face. She had blonde hair and was wearing a cinnamon-colored blouse and green slacks. Her petrified green eyes locked onto Athena. "Please!" she pleaded. "Help me!"

Athena went to rise, but Grizzly grabbed her left arm and restrained her.

"Don't," he cautioned.

"I should help her!" Athena insisted.

"There's nothing you can do," Grizzly told her. "They'll kill you if you interfere."

Corpus glanced at them. "Move aside!" he commanded with a sweep of his right arm.

Grizzly rose and pulled Athena to the right.

Polidori, Minshi, and the three Vampires arrived at the table with their victim.

"God! Help me!" the young woman cried desperately. She was lifted into the air and deposited on her back on top of the table. Working in concert, the Vampires strapped her wrists and ankles. "Help me!" she screamed.

The banquet hall was a madhouse. Shrieking and sobbing, the captives from Aguanga resisted the Vampires in vain. One by one the prisoners were firmly bound to the wooden tables. The Vampires remained emotionally calm through the bedlam, many licking their lips or exposing their pointed teeth in mocking grins.

Corpus hammered on the bell again after all of the captives were properly restrained. He faced the expectant Vampires and smiled. "Brothers and sisters, feeding time is here! You know the rules. Until the day comes when there is an abundant supply, we must share the foodstuff."

The prisoners had fallen silent at the sound of the golden bell. They listened to the Vampire leader with fear in their eyes.

"No gorging. No quarreling," Corpus went on. "We must be civilized about this," he added sarcastically.

Some of the Vampires laughed.

"I want to leave!" Athena declared.

Corpus looked at her. "Leave? How can you be so rude?"

"I don't want to see you kill these people!" Athena stated.

Corpus grinned. "Who says we're going to kill them?"

"You're not?" Athena responded, perplexed.

"We don't kill our foodstuff outright," Corpus elaborated. "We milk them for all they are worth."

Athena stared at the terrified woman on the table. "Do you mean . . ."

"Exactly," Corpus said with a smirk. "Observe and learn." He turned and tapped the bell twice.

The man in white promptly appeared. "You rang, sir?"

"Yes, William," Corpus said. "Bring the tray."

"At once," William replied. He hurried through the door in the rear wall.

"Why are you making me watch this?" Athena asked.

"The experience should be educational," Corpus told her. "For both of you."

"That works both ways," Grizzly interjected.

Corpus glared at the bear-man. "What does that mean?"

"You've got an education coming," Grizzly said. "Sooner than you think."

"Are you threatening me?" Corpus demanded.

Grizzly shook his head. "No," he said solemnly. "It's a promise."

Corpus leaned on the table. "Pay close attention to the festivities, fool. Your turn isn't far off."

"Dream on," Grizzly quipped.

The man in white returned bearing a large silver tray laden with an enormous pile of odd items. He dutifully placed the tray on the table in front of the Vampire leader, then departed.

"You may find these interesting," Corpus remarked. He picked up a thin, clear plastic tube or hose approximately a foot in length. One end of the tube was open, but the other was capped by a small needle. "Do you know what this is?"

"It looks like an intravenous tube," Athena commented.

"And it is," Corpus confirmed. "We appropriated cases of these from a hospital in Palm Springs. They make our feeding much easier. Originally, our ancestors drank the blood from vials. Later we experimented with straws." He wagged the tube. "And now we have the ideal method."

The young woman groaned.

"Please," Athena said, "I don't want to watch this."

Corpus chuckled. "Too bad."

"Why don't you feed on animals?" Athena asked. "Why use humans? This is barbaric. It's sick!"

"Who are you to judge us?" Corpus retorted. "And to answer your question, we do feed on animals for variety. But it's not the same. We prefer the sweet, delicious taste of humans. Females taste the best."

Athena stared at the young woman in despair.

Corpus handed a second feeding tube to Loring, then slid the tray across the table to Polidori and Minshi. Each Vampire took one of the feasting utensils. The tray was passed to the other Vampires, from one table to the next.

Many of the captives were weeping. Some cursed the Vampires.

The young woman on the head table glanced at Athena. "What's your name?"

"Athena Morris."

"I'm Greta Hogue from Aguanga," Greta said. "If you manage to get out of here, please tell my parents and brother you saw me."

Athena felt a congestion in her throat and swallowed.

Greta closed her eyes, her lips shaping soundless words.

The tray was still making the rounds.

Grizzly was in an emotional quandary. He wanted to tear into the Vampires, to feel his claws ripping their bodies apart. But any aggressive act on his part would undoubtedly result in Athena's death. Her life was his paramount consideration, and he refused to recklessly endanger her.

Greta Hogue suddenly opened her eyes and gazed at the bear-man. "I can tell you don't like the Vampires. Will you help me?"

Grizzly spread his hands in a helpless gesture. "What can I do? There are too many."

"A glimmer of intellect," Corpus quipped. "There's hope for you yet."

Greta's face was unspeakably sad.

His shoulders slumping, Grizzly bowed his head and stared at the tiled floor. What should he do? Aid this girl and get Athena and himself killed? To help her would be suicidal. Besides, she was a human, and he was not excessively fond of humans. Except for Athena. But if he stood there and did nothing, how would he feel later? He wasn't like Blade; he didn't believe in all that Spirit nonsense. He relied on his conscience to dictate his actions, to determine between right and wrong. Was it right for him to stand there and do nothing?

Corpus surveyed the chamber. "Everyone has a feeding tube. We can continue." He raised his arms. "Brothers and sisters! Enjoy yourselves!"

Grizzly looked up.

The Vampire leader leaned over Greta Hogue, examining her left arm. He traced his right index finger across her skin and she shivered. "You have fine veins, my dear."

Minshi, Polidori, and the vampiric conclave watched him intently, hungrily.

"This won't hurt much," Corpus told Greta. "The needle may sting a bit."

Greta closed her eyes again. "Please! Don't!"

"Quit whining, bitch," Corpus snapped. He aligned the needle over a bluish vein on the inside of her elbow.

"No!" Greta cried.

Corpus unexpectedly glanced at his second in command, Loring. "Why aren't they here yet?"

Loring's hooked nose bobbed as he did a double take. "Who?"

"The giant and his crew," Corpus said. "I gave orders for them to be captured and brought here. Why haven't they arrived?"

Loring shrugged. "Maybe Nordier, Prest, and the rest took longer than we expected to catch up with the giant."

"And perhaps they ran into trouble," Corpus commented. "Take ten men and go find them."

"Now?"

"Now," Corpus said.

Loring looked at Greta, the tip of his tongue visible between his red lips. "But we're just about to feed!" he complained.

Corpus straightened, his features shifting, becoming bestial. "When I give you an order," he growled, "you will obey it! You will leave now!"

His disappointment obvious, Loring dropped his feeding tube on the table and headed off.

"Pick any ten to go with you," Corpus instructed. "And if they object, they can lodge their protest with Minshi."

Loring walked toward the front doors, pointing at Vampires at different tables, selecting ten to accompany him. Not one lodged a protest.

Corpus waited until Loring and company were gone and the doors were bolted, then he lowered himself above Greta, leering maliciously. "And now, my dear, a truly exquisite experience is about to be yours. Your blood, your essence, will nourish us. And for this treat, we thank you."

Tears welled from Greta's eyes.

True to his word, and ever so gently, Corpus slowly inserted the needle into her vein.

Greta flinched and gasped.

Corpus pinched the plastic tube near the needle to prevent the blood from flowing until he was ready. He insured the needle was fully inserted, then stroked her arm with his left hand. "How beautiful," he said softly.

"Corpus! Don't!" Athena pleaded.

The Vampire leader didn't bother to look at Athena. "If you open your mouth again," he warned, "Minshi will separate your head from your shoulders with his bare hands."

Minshi grinned.

Grizzly caught Athena's eye and shook his head.

"Are you ready, my dear?" Corpus asked Greta. He raised the open end of the tube to his mouth, his lips puckering as they enfolded the clear plastic, and released the pressure near the needle.

Greta Hogue fainted.

His lips moving out and in, as if he was kissing someone, Corpus sucked on the tube as the blood flowed upward. He sighed contentedly when the crimson fluid reached his mouth, savoring the taste, his eyes becoming dreamy with rapture.

The assembled Vampires took their cue from their leader. They inserted needles into the captives and began feeding with undisguised relish.

Athena was unable to turn aside. She was stunned by the grisly scene, her loathing overwhelming.

Minshi and Polidori were eager to quench their thirst, Polidori taking Greta's right elbow as Minshi reached down and gripped the bottom of her right slacks leg. He hardly seemed to strain as he ripped the fabric from the hem to the crotch. Saliva coating his lips, he draped the split material on either side of her leg. Methodically, with total concentration, he inserted his needle and began feasting in great gulps, blood spilling out the corners of his mouth.

"Dear Lord!" Athena mumbled in dismay.

The banquet hall was filled with sucking and slurping sounds as all of the Vampires started feasting. Some of the captives thrashed futilely, others became hysterical, blubbering and babbling, while more than a half-dozen succumbed to shock.

Dizziness flooded Athena's mind. She clutched at the nearest chair for support, and then Grizzly was there, his right arm around her slim shoulders.

"I'm here," he said.

"I can't stand this!"Athena stated. "It's . . . obscene! And they plan to do it to us!"

"I won't let them," Grizzly assured her.

"How will you stop them?"

Grizzly didn't answer. He couldn't answer. Because there was no answer.

# CHAPTER SIXTEEN

**B**oone was standing over a pair of dead Vampires when his companions arrived at the junction.

"Are you all right?" Blade asked, scanning the intersecting corridors for more of the fiends.

"Fine," Boone responded. He prodded one of the Vampires with his M-16, satisfying himself the creature was deceased.

"What happened?" Blade queried.

"They appeared down the hall to the right," Boone explained. "I tried to follow orders and return to warn you, but they ran like the wind. They were at the junction before I went ten feet. I didn't have any choice."

"From here on out we move as fast as we can," Blade directed. "Those shots were bound to be heard. We must locate Grizzly and Athena before reinforcements arrive."

"How will we find them, sir?" Sergeant Havoc questioned.

"We just keep looking," Blade said. "Thunder, the rear. I'll take point. Boone, stay close to Havoc. He twisted his left ankle. Help him if he slows up."

"I don't need a baby-sitter," Havoc declared.

"This isn't a debate," Blade reminded him.

Sergeant Havoc frowned but stifled his disapproval.

"Move out," Blade said. He took the right branch, proceeding at a brisk walk, wanting to put a lot of distance between the two corpses and the Force. Prest had claimed there were hundreds of Vampires inhabiting the Heartland. If so, where were they? He was mystified by their absence. The Force had encountered only a handful, and the rest had to be close by.

But where?

He came to another intersection and paused, waiting for the others.

"Which way?" Boone inquired.

Blade glanced at the noncom. "How are you holding up?"

"No problem," Sergeant Havoc replied.

"Okay. We go straight," Blade directed, then led off. A lantern ahead revealed more of the same: an empty corridor with wooden walls and a dirt floor. A door appeared to his left and he angled toward it. His right hand gripped the knob and turned, and he was surprised to discover it wasn't locked. Inside were stacks of boxes and crates.

"Anything?" Boone asked.

Blade shook his head and resumed his search. At the next intersection he took a left. At the one after that a right. His frustration was mounting with every stride. He now believed that he'd committed a major mistake by venturing into the Vampires' sanctum. The network of passages was bewildering; a person could seemingly wander in them forever.

A junction materialized 40 feet in front of him.

What was that?

Blade stopped and crouched, his eyes narrowing as he scrutinized the junction. Vague, pale forms were moving through it. Vampires! He counted ten or eleven, his finger on the M-16's trigger, expecting to be spotted at any moment. But the party of bloodsuckers never noticed him. He received the impression they were in a hurry. Prudence was necessary, so he counted to 20 before rising and advancing to the intersection. A quick glance to the right confirmed the Vampires were gone. Relieved, he stepped from concealment.

Boone, Sergeant Havoc, and Thunder joined him.

"Did you see them?" Blade whispered.

Boone nodded. "Do we go after them? They could lead us to Athena and Grizzly."

"Too risky," Blade said. "Their senses are better than ours. They may spot us. Let's see where they came from." He marched into the left fork.

This corridor was unusual. Two lanterns were attached to the walls instead of one. The dirt was well trampled, indicating the hallway was used frequently. A row of doors lined both sides and a few were open.

Blade stared at the first door to his right, and he was startled to see light emanating from the doorway. He cautiously approached to within a yard, the M-16 leveled.

Without any warning, a woman stepped from the room. She was a brunette, her shapely figure clad in a brown loincloth and a strip of leather across her large breasts. Her brown eyes widened at the sight of the giant. "Who are you?" she blurted out loudly.

"Keep your voice down," Blade advised. "We're here to help you."

"Who are you?" she repeated.

"We're from the outside," Blade said. "We're going to rescue you."

"Like hell you will!" the woman said.

"What?" Blade asked, not certain he'd heard her correctly.

"I'm not leaving Heartland, mister," she stated.

"Why not?"

"I like it here," she said.

"Have the Vampires brainwashed you?" Blade queried.

"Give me a break!" she responded indignantly. "I want to stay because I have it real good here. I'm Loring's squeeze and he treats me like a princess."

"I don't understand," Blade admitted.

"I understand, sir," Sergeant Havoc commented from the Warrior's rear. "This woman is nuts."

"Loring is my mate," she disclosed. "I won't leave him. I can't."

"You're in love with a Vampire?" Blade inquired in amazement.

"Lots of the Venesects have human mates," she said. "It's not that unusual."

"And what do you think will happen down the road?" Sergeant Havoc demanded. "Will this Loring love you forever or just as long as it suits his purpose?"

"He does love me," she insisted. "He'd never hurt me. He's treated me special from the day he took me from my home in Fallbrook."

"Did you have a family?" Blade asked.

"A husband," she replied. "A foul-mouthed, alcoholic, wife-beater. Compared to that son of a bitch, Loring is a swell guy."

"Loring is a Vampire," Havoc remarked. "Vampires drink human blood."

"And humans kill animals for food," she retorted. "We eat their meat and drink their blood."

"Humans don't drink animal blood," Havoc said.

"Oh? Haven't you ever eaten a raw steak?" she countered.

"Are you positive you won't come with us?" Blade pressed her.

The brunette shook her head, sadness tinging her features. "I can't."

"You won't," Havoc said.

"I can't," she repeated. "I'm pregnant."

For a moment no one said a word.

"I'll have to ask you to go back in your room," Blade stated. "I can't let you warn the Vampires. We'll tie you up and gag you, but I'm sure someone will free you before too long."

The brunette looked into his eyes. "I can't let you do that," she said softly. Without any warning, she whirled and dashed down the corridor. "Help! Help! The Heartland is under attack!"

"Damn!" Blade fumed, starting in pursuit.

Boone darted past the Warrior, his lean legs flying. He overtook the brunette within ten feet. She looked over her left shoulder, about to shout again. Boone slammed the stock of his M-16 against her head and she sprawled onto the floor. He clubbed her again when she tried to rise.

More humans appeared, gaping at the Force members and the unconscious brunette.

Blade realized the entire corridor was occupied by the human mates of the Vampires. He didn't see any of the ghouls, but they had to be nearby. "In your rooms!" he bellowed, waving the M-16 as he jogged ahead.

The men and women promptly obeyed, door after door swinging shut.

"Now what?" Boone questioned as the Warrior came abreast.

"We haul butt," Blade advised. Taking the time to bind all of the humans would be impractical. He ran toward a junction at the far end of the hall.

A human male in a brown loincloth emerged from a door on the left, a hatchet in his left hand. "Stop!" he cried.

Blade shot him in the forehead, the single round propelling the man over a yard to crash onto his back. The Warrior sprinted past the body and reached the intersection without further interference. To his right was a dark passageway, to his left a hall containing several mesmerized humans who had heard the shot and were gawking at the giant in astonishment. Directly ahead was a well-lit, empty corridor. He went straight ahead.

Where in the world were all the Vampires?

The Warrior covered 50 yards. At the next junction he took a right, sticking to the passageways with the most illumination. The more illumination, he reasoned, the more human traffic. And the more human traffic, the more likelihood of Vampires also frequenting the area. He wanted to capture another Vampire and extract the whereabouts of Athena and Grizzly. But he had to find a few Vampires first, the fewer the better, making a capture easier.

The Vampires, however, found the Force sooner, and there were more than a few.

"Blade!" Thunder suddenly called out. "We have company!"

Blade stopped and spun.

A pack of Vampires was bounding toward the Force. They had just turned the corner at the last junction, their faces grim, their speed incredible.

Blade counted six. He crouched and motioned for Boone, Thunder, and Sergeant Havoc to form a line across the corridor. Havoc was limping badly. Blade sighted on the pack 20 yards away, impressed by their courage. Unarmed, the Vampires were confronting four automatic rifles without a hint of fear. What else besides bravery would compel the six to make such a reckless assault when the Vampires must know the inevitable result? The Vampires were strong, their bodies immune to pain to a large degree, but they weren't invincible.

For a fleeting instant Blade admired them.

And then another motive abruptly occurred to him and he tensed. What if the Vampires were *not* acting recklessly? What if there was an ulterior motive to their frontal attack? These Vampires were coming from the corridor the Force had vacated moments ago. Was it possible this was the same party he'd seen earlier? If so, there had been ten or eleven. Where were the rest? If the frontal charge was a ploy, then the rest must be . . .

Blade pivoted, his lips compressing at the sight of five more Vampires bearing down on the Force from the rear. They were less than seven yards distant and closing fast, their mouths open, their teeth exposed. "Behind us!" he shouted, and fired on full auto.

The Vampire nearest the right-hand wall was caught in the chest by the burst and hurled onto the floor, twitching and gurgling.

Boone twirled and cut loose, downing a second Vampire.

Thunder and Sergeant Havoc were concentrating their fire on the Vampires in front of them. Two of the six dropped soundlessly.

Blade shot another Vampire to the rear.

And then the two remaining Vampires were within six feet. Pouncing range. One came at the Warrior, the other hurtled at the Cavalryman.

Blade tried to swivel the M-16 barrel to shoot his opponent in the stomach, but the Vampire, a man with a hook nose and a cleft chin, swiped the barrel aside and clamped his hands on the Warrior's throat. Blade surged to his feet, astounded by the Vampire's strength. He could feel steely fingers digging into his neck. Releasing the M-16, he reached up and grabbed the Vampire's wrists, then attempted to pull those viselike hands from his throat.

Boone, meanwhile, was literally thrown for a loop. His foe gripped the M-16 and wrenched the weapon loose, tossing it to the floor with a contemptuous sneer. The Cavalryman went for his Hombres, but the revolvers were clearing leather when the Vampire seized the front of Boone's buckskin shirt with both hands and swept the Cavalryman up and over. Boone sailed over the Vampire's head and tumbled through the air before smashing onto his right side, dazed, the Hombres still clutched in his hands.

Without missing a beat, the Vampire lunged at Thunder, looping his right arm around the Flathead's neck and hauling Thunder backwards.

Sergeant Havoc suddenly perceived he was the only one firing. He shot one more in front, then twisted to see Blade grappling with one of their adversaries, Boone down, and Thunder being choked. He aimed at the Vampire choking Thunder.

Footsteps padded behind him.

Havoc never got off the shot. A white arm appeared over his right shoulder and tore the M-16 from his grasp. He attempted to turn, but a hand grabbed the back of his neck and hoisted him to his feet.

The last two Vampires closed on Blade.

The Warrior suddenly found himself the target of three Vampires. He saw them coming and managed to swing around, interposing the one with the hook nose between himself and the onrushing pair. Drawing his right arm back, he planted a tremendous blow on Hook Nose's chin. The Vampire, staggered, loosened his grip. Blade punched his foe a second time, his malletlike fist rocking the Vampire's head and causing Hook Nose to stagger back several feet.

Snarling and hissing, the last two Vampires bypassed Hook Nose and leaped, each gripping one of the Warrior's arms.

Blade's muscles bulged as he fought to fling the Vampires from him. They clung to him with all their might, but he was able to lift them from their feet and ram the one on his right into the wall. The Vampire started to sag. Before Blade could repeat the maneuver the battle was lost.

Hook Nose scooped up one of the M-16's and pointed the barrel at the giant. "Freeze or die!"

Blade's gray eyes flared and he hesitated.

"I mean it!" Hook Nose said. "I may want you alive, but I'll kill you and all of your friends if you don't do exactly as I say."

The Warrior observed Thunder in the grasp of a Vampire, on the verge of passing out. Sergeant Havoc was being held from behind by the neck and the right elbow, vainly endeavoring to swing his left elbow around and clip his captor.

"What will it be?" Hook Nose demanded.

Blade knew further resistance would be futile. He relaxed his arms in resignation.

"That's better," Hook Nose said. "What's your name?"

"Blade."

"I'm Loring."

"My displeasure, I'm sure."

"Save your insults," Loring stated. He looked at the Vampire holding Blade's left arm. "Collect their weapons and packs."

Blade, Havoc, and Thunder were stripped of their backpacks, guns, and knives. The Vampire finished frisking Thunder, who was lying on his back on the floor, and glanced up. His forehead creased as he gazed down the corridor. "Wasn't there another one?"

The Vampire responsible for subduing Thunder turned. "Yeah. There was a guy in buckskins. I took him down."

"He must be hiding in one of the rooms down the hall," the first Vampire commented. "Should we look for him?"

Loring reflected for a moment. "No. We don't want to keep Corpus waiting. You know how impatient he can become, and what happens when he loses his temper. We'll take these three to the banquet hall. I'll send a detail back here to find the guy in buckskins. He's just one human. He can't do much harm."

The Vampires let go of Blade and Havoc. Loring covered the giant and the soldier while his companions gathered the gear. One of the Vampires slung Thunder over his right shoulder.

"Let's go," Loring said. "I'll tell you the way. And remember, we're right behind you. Go straight, the way you came."

Blade complied, Havoc at his side.

"I can't believe Boone ran out on us," the noncom remarked.

"You know Boone better than that," Blade declared.

"We've made a mess of this mission, haven't we, sir?" Sergeant Havoc mentioned.

"That's the understatement of the decade," Blade responded

bitterly.

Sergeant Havoc's lips curled downwards as he limped along.

"How's the leg?" Blade inquired.

"Worse than ever."

"No more talking!" Loring snapped.

They walked a dozen yards in silence.

"Hey!" Loring said. "I want to know something."

Neither Blade nor Havoc responded.

"Didn't you hear me?" Loring demanded.

"You said not to talk," Blade replied.

"Very funny," Loring commented. "I want to know which one of you slugged Bernice?"

"Bernice?" Blade said.

"My mate. One of you bastards knocked her out. She was on her knees when I found her. Which one of you is responsible?"

Blade and Havoc ignored the question.

"That's okay. Play your little games," Loring said. "I'll find out which one, and when I do, you'll pay! I think I'll peel strips of skin from your body and watch you beg for mercy."

Sergeant Havoc glanced at Blade and grinned. "What a swell guy!"

# CHAPTER SEVENTEEN

The grand feast was winding down.

A majority of the Vampires had finished feeding and were seated in their chairs, their expressions serene, their eyes placid, their mouths rimmed with a red film. The captives from Aguanga, weakened by the sudden loss of pints of blood and emotionally ravaged by their traumatic ordeal, scarcely moved. They moaned and groaned pitiably, trickles of blood seeping from the puncture marks left by the needles.

Corpus sat in his chair at the head table, leaning back, his arms draped at the sides of his chair, his eyes glassy, a twisted smile conveying his contentment.

Minshi and Polidori, sitting across from Corpus, were equally satiated.

Grizzly and Athena were two of the few still standing. His right arm encircled her shoulders. "I'm sorry," he said.

"What are you sorry for?" Athena asked weakly. Her shoulders were slumped, her chin on her chest, tears moistening the corners of her eyes.

"I should have done something," Grizzly stated softly.

"There was nothing you could do," Athena said, disputing him, sniffling.

Grizzly gazed at the limp, crimson-speckled women and men on the tables and frowned, his eyes focal points of torment. When he spoke, his words were barely audible. "I was wrong. I should have tried to save them."

"You would have been killed," Athena said.

"Probably," Grizzly agreed. "But I'm a member of the Force. I'm pledged to protect the people from every Federation faction. I volunteered to serve. No one forced me." He sighed. "I've learned a valuable lesson here today. We can't turn from our responsibilities. We can't shirk our duties. We have to try, no matter what the cost. There's no way of knowing if we'll succeed or not, but failure isn't the same as shame. True shame comes from not trying. Do you see my point?"

Athena looked at him in respect. "Yes, I do."

Grizzly stared at Greta Hogue. Her eyes were fluttering, her breathing ragged, and periodically she uttered a feeble whine. "Too bad for her that I learned my lesson too late."

A sarcastic snicker sounded from the other side of the table. "How pathetically noble!" Corpus cracked.

Grizzly glared at the Vampire leader.

"Spare us your sentimental garbage!" Corpus stated. "You're fooling no one but yourself. Face facts."

"What facts?" Grizzly responded.

Corpus smirked. "You're a coward."

Athena could see Grizzly's jaw muscles twitching as he removed his arm.

"I'm not a coward," Grizzly said.

"You didn't even make an attempt to help these wretches," Corpus declared. "And you have the gall to talk about your responsibility? Hypocrite."

Athena expected Grizzly to fly across the table in a fit of rage; instead, he bowed his head, his body sagging.

"You know I'm right, don't you?" Corpus gloated.

A hard pounding on the front doors brought an end to the conversation.

"Open the doors!" Corpus bellowed.

Two Vampires moved sluggishly to the huge doors and slowly undid the bolts.

Athena thought she would swoon.

Blade and Sergeant Havoc entered the banquet hall, Havoc hobbling on his left foot. Escorting them were five Vampires, including Loring. One of the Vampires was carrying Thunder. There was no sign of Boone.

Grizzly had turned as the doors swung wide. His face lit up at the sight of his colleagues.

"More company, I see," Corpus said, rising. He nodded at Minshi and Polidori, both of whom rose and stepped to the left, studying the new arrivals. Minshi seemed particularly interested in Blade.

"You apprehended them. Good," Corpus remarked as Loring's party neared the head table. "But weren't there four of them?"

Loring walked to the right, past the Warrior and the soldier. "Yes. One got away. But he can't get far. I'll send a search squad after him right now."

"See to it," Corpus instructed. "Lead them personally."

Loring hastened toward the tables on the left side of the chamber.

"I am Corpus," the head Vampire announced.

"Whoop-de-do," Sergeant Havoc quipped.

Corpus ignored the soldier and stared at the giant. "Your name, sir?"

The Warrior was surveying the room in dumbfounded stupefaction. His eyes roved over the victims of the gruesome blood feast, his lips slightly parted.

"Your name, sir?" Corpus repeated.

The Warrior's burning gaze shifted to the Vampire. "You're the one responsible for this?"

"I can't claim all the credit," Corpus said humbly.

"I hope you can count," Blade said.

Corpus seemed puzzled. "Why?"

"Because your days are numbered."

Surprisingly, Corpus laughed. "I appreciate a sense of humor. But you still haven't told me your name."

"Blade," the Warrior disclosed.

"What an odd name," Corpus commented.

The Vampires carrying the backpacks and weaponry stepped forward. "The name fits," one of them said. "You should see what he was packing.''

"Show me," Corpus directed.

Relieved at being able to deposit all the gear on the table, they piled the backpacks, M-16's, knives, and 45's in a heap. One of them held aloft the Bowies, one in each hand, then set them down.

Corpus whistled. "You go in for big knives."

"The better to gut you with," Blade said.

Corpus chuckled. "A luxury you shall never enjoy."

Blade glanced at Athena and Grizzly. "Are you two okay?"

"Fine," Athena replied.

Grizzly didn't answer.

"Who sent you?" Corpus asked the giant. "Why are you here?"

"To exterminate the Vampires," Blade answered bluntly.

"Never happen," Corpus said. He gestured at one of the chairs across from him. "Have a seat and I'll tell you why."

The Warrior stood still.

"Why engage in this childish behavior?" Corpus asked. "I could have you killed now. All of you! But I have better plans for you, and I'm offering my hospitality. If there is more than solid muscle between those ears of yours, you will graciously accept. Unless," he said and leaned on the table, "you want to antagonize me and spoil my mood. In which case I might change my mind and exterminate some of *you* right this instant." He looked at Athena as he spoke.

Blade reluctantly walked to the table and stood behind the chair.

"Make room for them," Corpus commanded, sitting.

Several other Vampires relinquished their seats.

"All of you! Sit down!" Corpus instructed the giant's associates. "You must be hungry. I will have food brought."

"I won't be able to eat for a week," Athena mentioned as she took a seat.

Grizzly sat down next to her.

Sergeant Havoc moved to Blade's left, waited for the Warrior to sit, then eased into a chair, keeping his left leg as straight as possible.

Corpus pointed at the Indian. "Revive him."

One of the Vampires held the Flathead as a second slapped his cheeks lightly. Thunder took a deep breath and his brown eyes opened.

"Join us," Corpus stated, indicating a chair to the soldier's left.

Manifestly confused, not quite fully recovered, Thunder stumbled to the wooden chair and sat, his questioning gaze on Blade.

"How cozy," Corpus quipped. "Would you care for your food now?"

"No thanks," Blade replied.

"It won't be poisoned," Corpus said. "I assure you."

"No thanks," Blade reiterated.

"I see you possess an obstinate streak," Corpus mentioned. "Very well. Suit yourself. Just remember this was your idea when morning arrives and you're famished."

"Why are you toying with us?" Blade asked.

"Who's toying?" Corpus retorted. "Can't your dim intellect conceive of a higher purpose to my curiosity? A person in my position makes many enemies. In order to survive, I must grow to understand my enemies as well as I understand myself. Ignorance breeds weakness."

"What will you do to us?" Blade inquired.

"Please, let's dispense with morbid affairs," Corpus responded. "The aftermath of a feeding invariably results in a euphoric high. I like to savor the sensation." His eyes narrowed in contemplation. "Now about exterminating the Venesects—"

"You will be annihilated," Blade said, interrupting. "It's inevitable."

"Nothing in life is inevitable except dying," Corpus said. "And the Venesects will never die out. We're here to stay."

"Your time is running out. Sooner or later the California Army will invade the Dead Zone with a battalion or more. You won't stand a chance," Blade stated.

"You exaggerate, my friend," Corpus disputed the giant. "There are endless passages under the Heartland, and only the Venesects know every one. If an army invaded, we would see them coming miles off. We would secret ourselves and never be found. They could try bombing us or using artillery, but this far underground we wouldn't even be fazed. And if, for the sake of argument, they successfully launched a sneak attack and penetrated the Heartland, they wouldn't kill all of us. Some of us, you can be sure, would escape. And those who did would perpetuate our bloodline through the millennia.''

"You have this all thought out," Blade noted.

Corpus smiled. "I try." He thoughtfully considered the giant. "So who sent you? The governor of California?"

"I'm not at liberty to say," Blade replied.

"How rude," Corpus declared. "And here I am, trying to be so polite. My major flaw is my excessive kindness."

Blade pointed at the woman on the table. "You call this kindness?"

"No. She comes under the category of tasty treats," Corpus said, then laughed.

"Her name is Greta Hogue," Athena interjected. "She's from Aguanga."

Greta Hogue! Ethan's sister! Blade stared at her, realizing she was in shock.

"Do you know her?" Corpus asked.

Blade shook his head.

"I think you're lying," Corpus stated. "And I weary of your arrogance! You cease to amuse me! I have changed my mind. Dawn is several hours off. You have until one hour before daylight!"

"What happens then?" Blade questioned.

Corpus grinned wickedly. "Some of us will enjoy a snack before retiring for the day!"

# CHAPTER EIGHTEEN

The agony in his right side was slowly subsiding.

Boone leaned his back against the wall and closed his eyes. He hoped his ribs weren't fractured or busted. The pain would slow him down when it counted the most, when it came time to go after Blade, Thunder, and Havoc.

He couldn't wait much longer.

How long had he been in the darkened room? Boone wondered. He regretted temporarily leaving his friends, but he hadn't had any other choice at the time. That toss through the air had rattled him but good. He vividly recalled lying on the floor in intense anguish, his right side feeling numb. Rallying his strength, he'd looked up to see Thunder out of commission, Sergeant Havoc in the grip of a Vampire, and Blade on the verge of being subdued by three more of the bloodsuckers.

His right side lanced by exquisite spasms, and unable to shoot accurately, he'd done the only thing he could: saved himself so he could later save them.

Boone remembered forcing his body to move, to roll away from the fight, simply intending to put some distance between the Vampires and himself. His action had been instinctive, not predicated on any clever scheme. When the open doorway had

materialized on the right side of the corridor, he'd immediately
rolled into the unlit room and collapsed, the torment in his right
side almost unbearable. He'd waited with baited breath for the
Vampires to find him.

Amazingly, they hadn't come.

Boone had listened to the Vampires depart with his
companions. He'd overheard the comment the one called Loring
had made about sending a detail to locate him, and he wasn't
about to wait around for them to arrive.

Maybe he could manage now.

Boone opened his eyes and struggled erect, using his elbows
to brace himself as he rose. With a firm grip on the Hombres,
he sidled to the doorway and peeked outside.

The corridor was deserted.

Pleased his strategy was working, Boone stepped into the hall.
Which way should he go? The Vampires would likely expect
him to head for the hills, to continue away from the ambush
spot. They'd probably check every room, every hiding place,
beyond the site of the fight. But what about rooms in the opposite
direction, in the direction the Vampires had taken their
prisoners? Would the sons of bitches reckon on a frontal attack
from one man?

Not very likely.

Boone shuffled to the first junction, his stride increasing the
farther he went. The exercise was helping his side, reducing
the discomfort. He halted in the intersection and debated on the
proper branch. On a hunch he stuck with the corridor he was
in, going straight. At the next junction he took a right.

And froze.

Far off, someone laughed.

Boone jogged forward, seeking a door. He found one on the
left, holstered his left Hombre, and tried the doorknob.

Locked.

Undaunted, he proceeded another 15 feet and discovered a
door on the right. He grasped the knob and turned, grinning
in triumph when the door opened.

More laughter, but much closer.

Boone eased inside the dark room, listening for the telltale
evidence of an occupant, but all was quiet. He closed the door
until a crack afforded him a glimpse of the corridor.

Voices in conversation became audible.

". . . see the look on her face when I stuck the needle in her neck? I thought she'd shit her pants!"

"I hate it when they do that."

"I wish we didn't need to track down this bozo. I like to sleep after a feed."

"The foodstuff tonight was terrific."

"Ever tried to feed from a penis?"

"Once."

"What happened?"

"The prick pissed in my face."-

Feed from a penis? Boone aligned his eyes with the crack just as a party of Vampires walked past the door. He counted 12, and thought he recognized the one in the lead as one of those involved in the ambush. Loring maybe?

"Think we'll get to feed on the giant and his buddies?" a Vampire asked.

"Are you kidding?" responded another. "Corpus will save them for the inner circle."

"Quiet!" the leader barked.

Boone waited until he was certain the Vampires were long gone. He cautiously opened the door and looked both ways before stepping into the passage. The remark about feeding on a giant had alarmed him. So far as he knew, Blade was the only giant in the Heartland. Which meant the Vampires intended to feed on the Warrior, and soon. He resumed his hunt, listening intently.

What if he had miscalculated?

What if he reached Blade and the others too late?

He wouldn't be able to live with himself.

The fear of failing his friends motivated him to move faster. He passed door after door, and three junctions, without encountering anyone.

If only his luck would hold!

Boone was approaching an intersection when a tremendous commotion erupted ahead, as if dozens and dozens of people were talking at once. He took a sharp left at the junction, dashing to the first door on the right.

It was already open, and a lantern was visible on a wall to the left.

Boone ducked inside, then peered along the hallway to the junction. Vampires came into view, dozens of them. He quit tallying the number at 73 and estimated over a hundred filed through the intersection. Where were they all going? After him? He doubted they would send so many after one man. Were they on their way to a big shindig or coming from one? He stiffened as a small group appeared and headed in his direction.

No!

He closed the door and pressed his right ear to the panel.

". . . don't think it's fair," commented a Vampire.

"Tell that to Corpus and he'll let Minshi handle your complaint. You know what will happen then."

"I still don't think it's fair," the first one said. "Why should we be denied the privilege of feeding on those newcomers? Why should Corpus, Minshi, Polidori, and Loring receive special treatment? Aren't all Venesects created equal?"

"Some are more equal than others," the second Vampire stated.

Boone guessed the group was right outside his door.

"Corpus may be the best leader we've ever had," yet another Vampire remarked. "But one day he'll go too far. He's too dictatorial for my tastes."

"Don't let any of his friends hear you say that," advised a different one.

"I bet that giant has prime blood."

"And what about the mutant? Did you see his fur? I think he was cute." This voice sounded feminine.

"You would, Lamia."

"How would you find a vein through all that fur?" asked another male.

"You could always shave the fur off."

"Where there's a will, there's a way."

The voices trailed off as the group went beyond hearing range.

Boone knew the Vampires were referring to Grizzly. He was about to turn, to inspect the room, when someone else spoke sternly behind him.

"Who are you? No one is allowed in here!"

Boone was holding his right Hombre in front of his body at wasit level. He tightened his grip and glanced over his right shoulder, grinning broadly.

"Who are you?" repeated a man in a white shirt, pants, and apron.

"Howdy," Boone said. Five feet separated the two, and he wanted the man to move a little closer before making his move. Plugging the guy was out of the question; the Vampires would hear the shot.

"Does Corpus know you are in here?" the man asked belligerently.

"Of course he does," Boone lied, scanning the room. He recognized he had stumbled into a large kitchen; pots and pans were stacked on shelves along the right wall, sturdy wooden tables spotted by bloodstains were in the center, and a pair of white sinks were in a corner on the left. On one of the wooden tables was an open cardboard case, and beside the case was a pile of strange clear tubes.

"I don't believe you," the man said. "What is your name?"

"Boone. I was sent to lend you a hand," Boone responded.

"Now I know you're lying!" the man in white declared. "I will inform Corpus of this intrusion." He pivoted and took a stride.

The Cavalryman took one bound and pounded the man in white on the back of the head with the Hombre revolver.

Staggering forward, the man clutched at the nearest wooden table. He shook his head in a vain effort to retain his mental clarity.

Boone wasn't about to give the fool a chance. He closed in and swung the revolver three more times. His first blow caught the man on the back of the head again; his second smacked into the right ear as the man tried to swivel and confront him; his third lashed the man across the temple, splitting the skin and drawing blood.

The man in white sprawled onto the white tile floor.

Boone took a deep breath and scrutinized the opposite side of the kitchen from the hall door. He spotted a stove in a corner to the right, and slightly to the left of the stove was a closed door.

What was on the other side?

He advanced to the door and gingerly tried the knob. It rotated easily enough, but as he went to open the door he heard voices from the far side.

Vampires?

Boone released the doorknob and pondered his next step. There were too many Vampires abroad in the corridors to risk continuing his search for the time being. The wise thing to do was to stay put. The guy in white was out for the count, and the kitchen, apparently, was off limits to most everybody. This would be a safe place to hole up for a spell.

But he couldn't take too long.

The lives of his friends were on the line.

# CHAPTER NINETEEN

An hour and a half before dawn.

Shadow and his five fellow braves were sleeping the slumber of deep exhaustion. The evening before they had finally found the missing half of their hunting party. Animals had nibbled at a few of the bodies, rendering the facial features on one of the dead braves indistinguishable and gnawing the fingers from two others. Awash in grief, Shadow and his companions had conducted the appropriate ceremonies to expedite the passage of the departed spirits to the realm of the Breath Giver. Hours were spent in digging graves, and then the weary braves had turned in, leaving one of their number on guard. But that worthy, seated next to the roaring fire, succumbed to his fatigue and dozed off, his chin on his chest.

Hours elapsed. Beginning to toss fitfully in his sleep, Shadow opened his eyes and gazed absently at the fire. He was lying on the ground ten feet to the rear of the guard, and everything looked as it should. Slipping into repose, he did not realize the sentry had fallen asleep until much later when he again opened his eyes and beheld the black man. For a minute he believed he was dreaming. Few blacks lived near the land of his people, and Shadow had encountered them only a few times when on trips to the towns of the whites. This one was a huge black, almost as big as the white giant called Blade, very muscular, dressed in a brown leather vest, brown pants, and black boots.

"Hi, there," the black said with a smile. He was crouching an arm's length from Shadow, an M-16 cradled in his arms.

Shadow started to rise, and suddenly the barrel of the M-16 was nearly touching his nose.

"Do it slow, my man," the black advised. "Real slow. I'm not alone." He gestured with his left arm.

Shadow was startled to see dozens of somber men ringing the camp, all soldiers, all armed.

"Stand up," the black said. "Slowly." He stood.

"As you wish," Shadow stated, rising with his hands in the air.

"You can put down the hands, bro," the black said. "I ain't here to waste you."

The other braves were rousing from their sleep. Soldiers detached from the ring and stood over the braves with their M-16's extended. The sentry at the fire jumped up and was promptly covered by three automatic rifles.

"Behave yourselves and no one will be hurt," the black declared for everyone to hear.

"What do you want?" Shadow inquired.

"I'm lookin' for some friends of mine," the black said.

"What is your name?"

"Bear," the black said. "And yours?"

"I am Shadow."

"Well, Shadow, I'm sorry to disturb your beauty rest, but we need to talk," Bear stated. "I've been trampin' all over these woods searchin' for an outfit known as the Force. Ever heard of 'em?"

"No," Shadow said.

"You sure? Their leader is a big bozo by the name of Blade," Bear mentioned. "There are others with him. One is a cowboy I know called Boone. Another is an Indian, Thunder. There's a soldier, Sergeant Havoc. And a mutie named Grizzly and a woman named Athena."

Shadow nodded. "We ran into some of them."

Bear stepped closer to Shadow. "You have? When? Where? Which ones?"

"We saw them the day before yesterday, east of here," Shadow detailed.

"Where were they headin'?"

"Toward the Red Land. They said that one of them, a woman, had been captured by the Blood Drinkers," Shadow answered.

"The Red Land?" Bear repeated quizzically.

"The whites refer to it as the Dead Zone," Shadow explained. "But it is not dead. Many demons inhabit the Red Land, as do the Blood Drinkers, those the whites call Vampires."

"So you saw all of the Force except Athena?" Bear probed.

"I did not see a woman with them," Shadow replied. "Nor did I see a mutant."

Bear pursed his lips. General Gallagher had shown him photographs of each Force member he didn't know before his departure for Aguanga. Blade, of course, was an old friend. Boone too was a prior acquaintance. Bear had enjoyed the Cavalryman's company at the Home on several occasions, and the two had attended the summit meeting in Anaheim back in January. But Thunder, Havoc, Grizzly, and Athena were all new to him.

"They are your friends?" Shadow asked.

"Blade and Boone are," Bear responded. "I'm going to be joinin' up with them, but first I have to find them."

Shadow pointed at the row of freshly dug graves, at the mounds of dirt. "We will assist you, if you want. The Blood Drinkers killed some of our brothers."

"Sorry," Bear said. "I'd like to take you, but we need all our spare room on the Choppers for when we find the Force."

"Choppers?"

"Our helicopters. They're waiting to hear from me at Aguanga. I'm going to radio for them to pick us up and airlift us to this Dead Zone. Is there a big clearing around here?"

Shadow nodded to the south. "Two minutes from here."

"Good. It's about time these Vampires learned they can't be messin' with folks and gettin' away with it," Bear stated.

"May the Breath Giver preserve you," Shadow said.

"Huh? Yeah. Sure. Stay cool. And don't take no crap from the scuzzy lowlifes!"

Shadow watched the black and the soldiers melt into the trees, and he experienced a twinge of regret. He would have liked to get to know the black better. Bear was most . . . colorful. And the black employed a marvelous vocabulary.

What, for instance, were "scuzzy lowlifes."?

# CHAPTER TWENTY

"Where is Loring?" Corpus demanded impatiently. "I will not wait much longer! Dawn will break in less than an hour."

"He must not have found the one who got away," Polidori commented. "Knowing Loring, he won't return until he does."

"Then he will miss our bedtime snack," Corpus said with a sneer.

Blade shifted in his chair and stared over his left shoulder at the 20 Vampires gathered near the head table, awaiting the word from their leader. The Aguanga captives had been removed earlier, and Corpus had dismissed most of the Vampires, then spent his time expounding on how the Venesects would inevitably conquer the humans.

The Force members had listened in stony silence, with only Blade venturing to reply whenever Corpus became especially obnoxious. Obviously, the Vampire leader loved to hear himself talk. Blade had also used the time to study his associates, to gauge their readiness for what was coming. There was no way Blade would allow the Vampires to feed on his people without a fight, and while the Force was badly outnumbered, they could take a lot of Vampires with them.

Thunder took Corpus's diatribes in stride, his arms folded

across his chest. Sergeant Havoc had reacted passively, constantly rubbing his left leg, seemingly preoccupied with his injuries. Athena alternated between glaring at the Vampire leader and casting apprehensive glances at Grizzly. And Grizzly, quite uncharacteritstically, sat slumped in his chair in a dejected attitude.

Blade was perplexed by the hybrid's melancholy behavior. Normally, Grizzly was extroverted in the extreme. What could have transpired to so drastically modify his attitude? How effective would Grizzly be when the moment of truth came?

"Are you religious?" Corpus unexpectedly inquired.

Blade looked the Vampire in the eyes. "Yes."

"Then you will have a few minutes to make amends with whichever deity you worship," Corpus offered.

"The Spirit," Blade said.

"What?" Corpus said testily, as if he hadn't expected a response.

"Where I was raised, we believe in the dominance of the Spirit in our lives," Blade elaborated. "Living the will of the Spirit should be our paramount concern."

"Your Spirit must not reciprocate your devotion," Corpus said sarcastically. "Why doesn't this Spirit protect you? Where is this Spirit now, when you are on the brink of dying?"

"A person with genuine faith never dies," Blade declared.

Corpus laughed uproariously. Minshi and Polidori, standing to the left of the Warrior and slightly behind him, chimed in.

Blade idly stared at the pile of Force gear on the table in front of him, just out of reach. His Bowies were on the top of the heap. One lunge and they would be his.

"How can anyone believe all that religious gibberish?" Corpus said, mocking the Warrior. "Where was the God of all those Christian denominations—the Catholics, Presbyterians, Lutherans, and Baptists—when World War Three broke out? Where was the Allah of the Moslems? What happened to the Lord of the Quakers and the Mormons? Where was this God when all his precious children were having their buns fried to a crisp?"

"You misunderstand the nature of the Spirit," Blade remarked.

"How so?" Corpus asked. "Enlighten me."

Blade held his hands out, palms up. "Pick one."

Corpus did a double take. "What is this? Some childish game?"

"Pick one," Blade reiterated.

Corpus pointed at the giant's right hand. "There. So what?"

"So now you know why the Spirit did not intervene to prevent World War Three," Blade said.

"You're not making any sense," Corpus said.

Blade placed his hands on the edge of the table, slightly nearer to the pile of weapons. "You just exercised your free will, the same free will everyone has, the free will to live according to the will of the Spirit or to live according to the dictates of our own conscience, our own precepts of right and wrong."

Grizzly's head snapped up, and he cocked his head as he listened to the Warrior.

"If everyone lived consistent with the Spirit's will, if we all strived for perfection, if we all loved one another as the spiritual leaders of humankind have enjoined down through the ages, this world would be a Utopia," Blade asserted. "But very few live spiritual lives. They give lip service to the Spirit, then go their merry way. They allow their actions to be controlled by their fluctuating feelings, by their frame of mind at any given moment." His hands inched a fraction closer to the pile.

Corpus leaned forward. "Fascinating! I had no idea you are a religious fanatic. But tell me. How does this free-will business tie in with World War Three?"

"The Spirit bestowed on us the free will to make this planet a paradise or to destroy it," Blade said. "The choice is ours."

"A puerile assessment, if ever I heard one," Corpus remarked. He looked at Polidori. "I hope his blood doesn't contaminate ours with his stupidity."

Polidori cackled.

"I'll be damned!" Grizzly abruptly exclaimed.

Every face focused on the mutant.

"The coward speaks!" Corpus quipped.

"I think I understand you," Grizzly said to Blade.

"You do?" Blade responded.

"Yeah," Grizzly declared. "And now I know what I've got to do." His eyes narrowed. "Do you get my drift?"

Corpus glanced from the mutant to the giant and back again.

"Don't try anything foolish! You're outnumbered four to one."

Grizzly glowered at the Vampire leader. "I can count, asshole. And the odds are two to one."

"Oh?" Corpus rejoined, starightening. "You have allies I don't know about?"

"As a matter of fact, I do," Grizzly stated, slowly rising.

"Sit down!" Corpus commanded.

Grizzly raised his arms, tilting his forearms in the direction of the Vampire leader, his hands almost vertical. "Up yours!" he retorted, his fingers going rigid and locking in place, his five-inch claws sliding from under the flaps of skin behind each fingernail. He snarled, stepped onto his chair, and vaulted onto the head table, all in a quick, fluid motion.

"Stop him!" Corpus shouted, too late.

Grizzly launched himself through the air, slamming into Corpus's chest, the impact toppling the Vampire leader's chair backwards and sending them both to the floor.

Pandemonium erupted.

Minshi grabbed the tabletop, preparing to leap to his brother's assistance.

Blade came out of his chair in a rush, tackling the huge Vampire, and both went down, grappling for an advantage.

Sergeant Havoc, Thunder, and Athena started to grab for weapons from the pile of gear, but the 20 Vampires to their rear swarmed in. One grabbed Thunder's wrists, and another took hold of Athena. For a moment it seemed like their desperate bid for freedom was doomed.

Until an unforeseen wild card entered the fray.

A gunman named Boone, charging through the door in the rear wall, an Hombre in each hand. Both revolvers thundered once, and the Vampires gripping Thunder and Athena were each struck in the forehead and flung backwards. The Hombres boomed again and two more died.

For a few seconds the total attention of the 16 remaining Vampires was focused on the Cavalryman and his deadly guns.

Which was all the distraction Havoc, Thunder, and Athena needed. They snatched the handiest weapons from the heap: Thunder an M-16, Athena an M-16, and Havoc a pair of 45's. They swiveled, rising, and blasted away at point-blank range.

Wrestling with Minshi in a ferocious struggle on the floor,

Blade heard the gunfire and renewed his efforts to break loose and aid his friends. But the gigantic Minshi had other ideas. His left hand locked on the Warrior's throat, Minshi struck Blade a devastating blow to the chin. Stars exploded before the Warrior's eyes, and he doubled over as a knee drove into his groin.

Minshi growled and stood, pulling Blade after him. He effortlessly lifted the Warrior into the air, clear overhead, and hurled Blade onto the table.

Blade gasped as his left shoulder was jarred by the unyielding wood. Pain engulfed him. His head bumped an object and he twisted, his eyes brightening at the sight of the pile of Force gear, his Bowies now lying at the outer edge of the heap. He seized the knives and twisted onto his back.

Just as Minshi pounced, leaping onto the table top and diving at the Warrior.

Blade instinctively extended his arms, the Bowie tips straight out.

Minshi couldn't check his plunge. The Bowies caught him high on his chest, penetrating to the hilt, and he collapsed on top of the Warrior, his eyes quivering, wheezing.

Grunting with the effort, Blade tossed Minshi to one side, to the right, onto the table, and wrenched the Bowies out. He rose to his knees, his eyes flicking in all directions, assessing the battle. Ten of the Vampires were sprawled on the tile floor near the head table. Sergeant Havoc and Thunder were engaged in hand-to-hand combat, Thunder swinging his M-16 like a club, Havoc using his martial-arts skills against three Vampires as they tried to pin his arms. Athena was on the floor, straddled by a Vampire intent on choking the life from her. And Boone was frantically reloading his Hombres as a trio of Vampires scrambled over the tables toward him. Blade tensed his legs muscles, about to go to Athena's succor.

"Surrender or Corpus dies!" roared a raspy voice.

The Vampires abruptly ceased fighting, their eyes on the two figures on the far side of the head table.

Grizzly had his left hand, the claws retracted, encircling the Vampire leader's throat. The claws on his right hand were brushing Corpus's eyelashes. Slashes marked the Vampire's cheeks, chest, and arms, and rivulets of pink blood crisscrossed his torso. "Back off!" Grizzly barked. "Or I'll snuff this prick right now!"

Some of the Vampires complied. Others looked at their leader. "Do it!" Corpus ordered.

The ten Vampires backed away from the Force members.

Blade slid off the table and stepped to Athena's side. He replaced his left Bowie in its sheath and looped his left arm around her shoulders as she endeavored to stand, her knees wobbly. "I've got you," he said.

Grizzly looked at the Warrior. "You call the shots, boss man. What do we do?"

Blade was ever the realist, and his pragmatic side prevailed. "We get out of here and go for help. We'll take Corpus with us as insurance."

"What about them, sir?" Sergeant Havoc asked, nodding at the ten Venesects.

"We'll tie them up," Blade said. "It will buy us some time."

"Where's Polidori?" Grizzly queried. "I don't see that tittering idiot anywhere, and I know he was here when the fight began."

Athena straightened and pointed at the open front doors. "I saw him take off."

"He's going for reinforcements," Sergeant Havoc remarked.

"That's right!" Corpus gloated. "He'll come back with more Venesects than you can possibly handle! We'll rip you to pieces!"

Grizzly jabbed his claws into Corpus's right cheek. "If you open your mouth again, I'll cut out your tongue."

The Vampire leader clammed up.

"Okay!" Blade declared. "Grab your gear! We're leaving."

Moving with a sense of dire urgency, the Force members reclaimed their backpacks and weapons. They inserted fresh magazines into their M-16's and made sure their Colts were loaded.

Thunder slid an M-16 across the table to Boone, who slung the automatic rifle over his left arm, preferring to rely on his Hombres.

"All loaded?" Blade asked after a minute.

"All set, sir," Sergeant Havoc said. "Do you want me to tie these guys?"

"There's no time to waste," Blade said. He leveled his M-16 and fired. Only eight feet away, the Vampires had no time to charge and nowhere to flee. They were decimated on the spot, some screeching and flopping as they hit the floor. In seconds it was all over.

"You son of a bitch!" Corpus cried, enraged.

"Let's go," Blade said grimly, starting toward the huge doors.

"Wait!" Boone called. "We can skedaddle through the kitchen."

The Warrior glanced at the rear door. "Good idea. Over the tables! Move it!"

Thunder, Sergeant Havoc, and Athena climbed onto the tables, angling toward the kitchen door.

Blade followed them, watching the front.

Boone dashed to the rear door and threw it open, and only his superb reflexes saved his life.

The man in white was there, clutching a carving knife in his right hand, a maniacal expression contorting his face as he stabbed at the Cavalryman's chest.

Boone threw himself backwards, bumping into one of the tables, the Hombres at waist height. He thumbed back the hammer on the right revolver and planted a slug in the man's right eye, the force of the impact bowling the man in white over.

The Force members darted through the doorway, Blade bringing up the rear behind Grizzly and Corpus.

"You'll never get away with this!" Corpus snapped at the Warrior.

"I told you to shut your face!" Grizzly warned.

They reached the hallway, exited, and paused.

Blade glanced at Corpus. "Which way to the surface?"

"Go to hell!" Corpus replied.

"Grizzly," Blade directed. "Cut out his tongue."

"With pleasure!" Grizzly said, tapping the Vampire leader's lips with his claws.

Corpus stared into Grizzly's eyes for a moment, then looked at those razorlike talons. "Take a right."

# CHAPTER TWENTY-ONE

They emerged from the ruins near the east rim of the crater to find the sky filled with stars and a tinge of yellow lining the horizon.

"This is where we came in!" Sergeant Havoc exclaimed.

"How'd we get here so fast?" Boone questioned in disbelief.

"It pays to have someone who knows all the shortcuts," Athena said, glancing at Corpus.

Grizzly, standing behind the Vampire with his claws pressed against Corpus's neck, looked at the stark slag and girders to their rear. "And he isn't the only one. We're in for it now!"

Blade heard them too. The hubbub of many excited voices on their trail. The Vampires, not far off and closing.

"You won't escape!" Corpus boasted.

"To the rim!" Blade commanded. "Hurry!"

They raced to the crest of the crater. Sergeant Havoc, who had been hard pressed to keep up during the flight from the kitchen, practically dragged his left leg after him.

Blade stepped onto the rim and turned, his mouth a thin line as he surveyed the Heartland. "Leave Corpus with me and take off," he instructed them.

"Do what?" Grizzly responded.

"Did I hear you right?" Boone asked.

"You heard me," Blade said. "I'll hold them off as long as I can. Dawn is in ten minutes, and we know the Vampires can't tolerate the sun. If I can pin them there in the crater, you'll be able to escape."

"The noble sacrifice!" Corpus stated, and laughed.

"I'm not leaving you," Boone declared.

"Nor will I," Thunder concurred.

"None of us will," Athena said. "We're a team, right? The Force. We stick together through thick and thin."

Blade gazed affectionately at each of them. "I appreciate your sentiments. I really do. But this isn't the time to argue. Some of us must make it out of the Dead Zone. We've been down there. We know what's going on. We can bring an end to the reign of terror by getting word to General Gallagher. The Vampires must be stopped! Tell Gallagher to invade the Heartland with a regiment and all the firepower he can muster." He paused. "The lives of countless people depend on your getting through."

"I don't know," Athena said.

"Go!" Blade barked. "And that's an order!"

Athena looked at Grizzly. who nodded. She frowned, then started to the east.

Thunder gazed at the Warrior for a second before jogging after her.

"You too, Boone," Blade said.

The Cavalryman balked. "You're my friend."

"I am," Blade agreed. "And if you are really mine, you'll do as I say. Get."

Boone nodded once and took off after the others.

"Your turn, Sergeant Havoc," Blade remarked.

"No, sir."

Blade scrutinized the noncom. "*You* are disobeying a direct order?"

Sergeant Havoc sighed. "Not by choice. This leg of mine has had it. I can't go any farther, Blade."

"You could try."

"They'd overtake me, and you know it," Havoc said. "I'd rather make my last stand here."

Blade knew the noncom was telling the truth. "Okay. You can stay. But no sleeping on the job."

Havoc grinned and settled to the rim in a prone position.

"That leaves you," Blade addressed Grizzly.

"Forget it."

"I'm ordering you to leave."

"You're wasting your breath."

"Damn it, Grizzly! Listen for once!" Blade declared.

"No can do," Grizzly responded wistfully. "It's partially my fault we're in this fix. I'm seeing it through to the end."

"What are you talking about?"

Grizzly stared at the ruins. "A mutant's got to do what a mutant's got to do."

"You won't leave?"

"Nope. You can boot me off the Force later, if you want."

"Later then," Blade said, and faced the Heartland.

The babble of roiling voices was much louder.

Blade lay down a few yards from Sergeant Havoc and slanted his M-16 over the rim. "Wait until they're on the slope."

"Yes, sir," Sergeant Havoc said. He drew his right Colt and offered the automatic to Grizzly. "Here. You don't have a gun."

"I don't want one," Grizzly replied. "My claws are all I need. Thanks, though."

Corpus, standing on the rim to the right of Havoc, with Grizzly to his rear, gazed longingly at the inky contours of the Heartland. "Do you hear them? They'll be here soon. Do yourselves a favor and surrender while you have the chance."

"Do't make us laugh!" Grizzly retorted.

"You'll die here. You know that, don't you?" Corpus queried. "The three of you will be crushed like the gnats you are!"

Grizzly looked at Blade. "Can I shut this turkey up?"

Before Blade could respond, the Venesects poured from passages at the base of the ruins, streams of pale figures flowing into the crater and milling about.

"Which way?" one of them yelled to no one in particular.

"Up here!" Corpus suddenly shouted. "It's a trap!"

Grizzly plowed into Corpus from behind, his arms around the Vampire's thin waist, and together they pitched over the edge and tumbled down the slope.

"Grizzly!" Havoc cried.

The Venesects surged en masse toward the east side of the crater.

Frowning at his failure to terminate Corpus while he had the opportunity, annoyed because his arguments with the others had distracted him from his duty, Blade sighted on the leading row of Vampires and squeezed the trigger. There was no waiting for the Vampires to reach the slope, where Grizzly was now battling Corpus. The Vampires would overwhelm the mutant in an instant, and Blade was determined to see that they didn't. His initial burst took down over a half dozen, but it wasn't enough to slow them.

Sergeant Havoc joined in, his M-16 chattering, every shot connecting as he raked the front row. Five, six, seven Vampires toppled to the red dirt and the line wavered.

Blade continued firing, the white, scarecrow forms making excellent targets. He aimed at their heads, at the most vulnerable part of their anatomy, knowing a shot through the brain was the best bet to kill them. Eight more keeled over in half as many seconds.

Unnerved by the deadly fusillade, staggered by the loss of so many of their companions in the opening moments of the battle, the Vampires retreated into the passageways to regroup.

"They won't be so easy to stop the next time," Sergeant Havoc mentioned, replacing the magazine in his M-16.

Blade was engrossed in the fight on the slope.

Grizzly and Corpus were on their feet, exchanging a flurry of fist and claw blows, their postures awkward because of the incline. Corpus, taller and with the greatest reach, was landing powerful punches to the bear-man's face. In the banquet hall Grizzly had pinned the Vampire leader under the table, where Grizzly's shorter arms and claws had given him the close quarters advantage. But here on the open slope, able to maneuver and maximize his superior size, Corpus enjoyed the upper hand.

Backpedaling, Grizzly blocked a boxing strike intended for his throat. He was frustrated by his inability to land a lethal swipe of his claws and feeling exposed, perched on the incline with a horde of Vampires about to charge again at any second.

Corpus intuitively sensed his foe's trepidation and smirked. "This time the outcome will be different! No false bravado will save your hide!''

Grizzly ducked under another swing and backed up a step.

''A mutant's got to do what a mutant's got to do!'' Corpus mimicked the bear-man. ''What drivel! You're blaming yourself because you didn't even try to help those wretches from Aguanga.''

Astounded by his adversary's insight, Grizzly took another stride backwards. ''I am not,'' he said, but his tone lacked conviction.

''Who are you kidding?'' Corpus retorted, pressing his psychological attack. He realized the mutant was emotionally disturbed, a weakness he planned to exploit to gain the deceptive edge. ''Do you know why you didn't help them?''

Instead of responding, Grizzly lashed out with his right hand.

Corpus easily evaded the sluggish swat. ''Is that the best you can do?'' he taunted. ''It's not an answer to my question.''

Grizzly tensed, waiting for Corpus to come at him.

''I'll tell you the reason,'' Corpus stated derisively. ''You didn't help them because you're in love.''

''In love?'' Grizzly blurted out, inadvertently straightening.

Corpus coiled his leg muscles for the final spring. ''Yes! In love with that bitch Athena!'' he asserted.

The effect on Grizzly was worse than any physical blow could have been; his mouth slackened, his eyes widened, and he lowered his guard, his arms dropping to his sides. He was, for the space of a few seconds, thoroughly confounded and momentarily defenseless.

Which was exactly what Corpus wanted. He hissed as he sprang, digging his fingers in the mutant's neck and ramming his right knee into the bear-man's crotch. The momentum of his rush bowled the hybrid over, and they landed with Grizzly on his back and Corpus straddling his enemy's chest, his legs pinning Grizzly's arms to the ground. The Vampire leader's eyes blazed as he applied pressure on the throat, gouging his fingernails into the flesh. ''And now, you damn nuisance, we end this farce!''

Grizzly attempted to buck the Vampire off, without success.

''Did you really believe you would defeat the Venesects?'' Corpus scoffed. ''You pathetic fool! The Venesects are indestructible!''

Struggling to regain his composure, his self-control, Grizzly thrashed and tried to extricate his arms, squirming from side and side. He was experiencing difficulty breathing, and there was a tremendous pain in his chest and neck.

"When I'm done with you," Corpus declared, "I'll take care of those two morons on the rim!"

Grizzly tugged on his right arm, his concentration disjointed. What was the matter with him? Why couldn't he get his act together? Was it because he knew, deep in his heart, that the damn Vampire was right? His affection for Athena had prevented him from performing as he normally would. Anxiety over her safety had turned his resolve to mush, had tempered his feral intensity with debilitating indecision. Was the truth that hard to admit? What was so traumatic about being in love? Was it because Athena was . . . human?

Corpus, confident of victory, dug his nails in even more. "And then do you know what I'll do?" he demanded harshly. "I'll have your bitch tracked down and brought to me! Yes! And I'll feed on her myself! Just me! Wouldn't that be poetic justice?"

Corpus feed on Athena? Grizzly gritted his teeth and held his breath, saving what precious little air was left in his lungs, and jerked on his right arm.

"It's better this way," Corpus assured the mutant through taut lips. "The bitch and you would never have worked out! Can you imagine the monsters you'd breed?" He paused and sneered. "Funny, though. I've never heard of a mutant with the hots for a human piece of ass before!"

An inarticulate bellow of sheer rage burst from Grizzly's mouth. His right arm pulled free in a herculean effort, and he speared his claws up and in, burying them in the soft tissue under the Vampire's chin.

Corpus stiffened and grunted, then heaved himself backwards, tearing free of the claws, falling onto his back and rolling to the right. He rose, his left handing clutching at the punctures in his neck, his blood spraying over his fingers.

Grizzly was already erect. He roared as he took one bound and swiped his left hand across the Vampire's face, his claws ripping through Corpus's cheeks and nose, leaving stringy sections of dangling skin and lacerations oozing crimson gore.

Gurgling, in a panic, Corpus staggered backwards. He glanced at the Heartland and started to turn, to flee.

Grizzly wouldn't let him.

The mutant moved in close and drove his right claws into the Vampire's abdomen just above the loincloth. His right arm bunched, the muscles rippling under his fur as he tore his claws upward all the way to the sternum, effectively slitting Corpus open. Still in the grip of his blood lust, Grizzly drew both arms back, then lanced his claws into the Venesect's groin.

Corpus shrieked and beegan to sag, his right hand on his ruptured stomach, his left reaching lower.

With a savage twist, Grizzly yanked his claws from the Vampire's privates.

"No!" Corpus blubbered feebly as he sank to his knees, his left hand covering his crotch, his right endeavoring futilely to check the spilling of his internal organs as they gushed through the gaping slit in his abdomen. His intestines squished out and plopped onto the turf. "No!" he whined.

Grizzly stepped back and eyed the Vampire disdainfully.

His features a mask of torment, Corpus doubled over, then looked up at Grizzly in astonishment. "You . . . !"

Grizzly leaned down until his face was next to Corpus's. "You had me," he said, scowling. "No one has ever come closer to nailing me than you. But you blew it. You should never have mentioned Athena."

Blood poured from Corpus's mouth, spurting over his lower lip and down his chin.

"Funny, though," Grizzly said, mimicking the Vampire. "You were right. I do love Athena. But only you and I know it."

Corpus wobbled, his eyes glazing.

"I'd like to keep it a secret," Grizzly mentioned softly. "I'll never tell a soul. How about you?"

A convulsion racked the Vampire's body, he breathed one last, ragged breath, and pitched onto his face at the mutant's feet.

"I guess you won't tell anyone either," Grizzly remarked, gazing at the corpse. "Thanks. I appreciate that." He sighed, stared at the rim ten yards above him, then at the ruins.

Just as the Vampires launched their second attack.

# CHAPTER TWENTY-TWO

"What was that all about?" Sergeant Havoc asked as Corpus slumped to the dirt.

"I don't know," Blade said, his forehead creased in thought.

"What was all that talking they were doing?" Havoc queried. "I only caught a few words. Do you know what they were saying?"

Blade looked at the noncom. "I—" he began.

And a wave of Venesects poured from the demolished structures and raced toward the east rim.

The Warrior rose to his knees. "Grizzly! Get up here! We'll cover you!" he yelled.

Instead, Grizzly faced the onrushing Vampires.

"What the hell is he doing?" Havoc blurted. "He can't take them all on by himself!"

Blade raised his M-16 to his right shoulder. "Concentrate on those who get near to him. Give him some fighting room."

"He's crazy," Havoc declared, taking aim.

The Vampires were 20 yards from the mutant when Blade and Sergeant Havoc cut loose. With the steadily brightening sky now a pale blue, and the golden arc of the sun barely visible above the eastern horizon, the slope and the crater floor were bathed in a rosy light. The Vampires were perfect targets. Over a dozen in the center of the front of the wave, those barreling toward Grizzly, were killed in the first few seconds. As they fell, those to their rear bore to the left or the right, bypassing the bodies. Some went after the mutant, but the majority sprinted for the east rim.

Grizzly, crouching on the incline, went on the offensive, snarling as he charged. His claws flashing, his body a whirlwind, he met the Venesects head-on.

Blade saw the mutant shred a Vampire's throat, and then he was compelled to focus on the lines of white forms racing up the slope toward him. He sent a withering spray of lead into the foremost row.

Sergeant Havoc was likewise engaged, his marksmanship unerring. Vampire after Vampire dropped.

The left side of the wave abruptly changed direction, angling away from the giant and the soldier, heading for a point on the rim 20 yards off. Their strategy was clear. They would flank the two humans and come in from the side.

Blade pivoted, devoting his attention to the left flank. The magazine suddenly went empty and he swiftly ejected it and slapped home a new one. During Grizzly's fight with Corpus, Havoc and Blade had removed their spare magazines from their backpacks and crammed them into their pockets. The backpacks they had left lying on the rim.

The left side of the wave was almost to the crest.

Blade waited until 10 to 15 of the Vampires were just rising above the rim. He wanted them slightly off balance, in the act of stepping to the higher ground. At that precise instant he fired, sweeping the M-16 in an arc, going for their heads.

The ploy worked.

Outlined against the lightening sky, the leading line was silhouetted as they absorbed the rounds. Some screamed, others threw their arms in the air, and all except one was knocked backwards onto those scrambling up the slope. A domino effect toppled one after the other, dozens tripping over their companions, creating a jumble of legs and arms. The left flank was in confusion, their momentum checked.

Blade reached down and scooped his backpack into his right

hand, dropping the M-16. He pulled an explosive packet with a timer from the pack and swiftly adjusted the setting for one minute. The state-of-the-art packets could stop a tank cold. One was sufficient to blow a tank to smithereens, and Blade carried enough explosives in his backpack to destroy ten tanks.

Move! his mind shrieked.

He ran to the left, making for the rim above the floundering Venesects, holding the backpack and the packet at chest height.

Some of the Vampires saw him coming and tried to claw their way to the top.

Blade reached the edge directly above the mass of Vampires. He stuffed the packet into the backpack, then tossed the backpack overhand into the middle of the muddled bloodsuckers.

Move!

He spun and dashed toward Sergeant Havoc. "Hit the dirt!" he shouted, his legs pumping.

Havoc, striving to arrest the advance of the right flank up the slope, firing like a man possessed, glanced at the Warrior.

"Down!" Blade yelled.

The noncom promptly obeyed, diving onto his stomach.

Move!

His mind ticking off the seconds, Blade knew he had run out of time. He was in the process of leaping, attempting to put a few more feet between the slope and himself, when the detonator went off.

The explosion was stupendous, shaking the ground like an earthquake.

Blade felt the concussion slam into his back and he was flung for a loop, landing with a jarring impact.

For a moment the terra firma seemed to be airborne, as if the very planet was gasping in anguish. A colossal dust cloud soared heavenward, and seconds later the rain began, the pelting of red dirt and clumps of sod, the shower of pink droplets and body parts: severed arms and legs, decapitated heads, detached feet, and pieces of Vampire torsos.

Blade slowly stood, doubling over, the swirling dust stinging his eyes and causing him to cough. He squinted, covered his mouth with his left hand, and moved cautiously toward the rim. The dust obscured everything. He wasn't even certain he was heading in the right direction.

"Blade?" Havoc called out, not more than a yard distant.

The Warrior distinguished the noncom's crouching form in the billowing red dust. "Here!" he responded, stepping to the soldier's side and dropping to his knees.

"Where are the Vampires?" Havoc asked, craning his neck to the right and left. "I don't see them!"

"We'll have to wait for the dust to settle," Blade said, scanning the nearby ground for his M-16. He spotted the weapon lying at the edge and retrieved it.

"Did you see what happened to Grizzly?" Havoc questioned anxiously.

"No," Blade said, hoping the mutant had been far enough from the center of the blast to be spared.

They waited impatiently. The dust seemed to take forever to sink to the ground or disperse on the westerly breeze. Slowly visibility improved.

"I can see the right side!" Havoc exclaimed. "The Vampires are gone."

Blade swiveled to the left, his eyes narrowing.

A secondary crater now marred the slope of the great crater. Tendrils of smoke wafted upward. Blasted bits of pale bodies were everywhere. Piles of corpses served as a demarcation for the circumference of the explosion. A few Vampires still moved, twitching and groaning.

"There's Grizzly!" Sergeant Havoc stated.

Blade swung to the center.

Dozens of dead littered the slope and the ground below, and at the base of the incline was Grizzly, on his stomach, his arms outstretched, unmoving.

"Do you think he's—" Havoc started to say.

But the Warrior was in motion, sliding over the rim and speeding down the incline, covering yards with each stride, threading a path among the corpses, the M-16 in his left hand. He glanced at the ruins and saw no sign of the Vampires. Either the ghouls had thrown in the towel and were retreating into the bowels of the Heartland or they were reorganizing for yet another assault. For the moment, though, the coast was clear.

Lifeless Venesects encircled Grizzly in stacks two to four

bodies high. Each one bore testimony to the unbridled ferocity of the bear-man in the form of wicked claw marks; some had their throats slashed to shreds, some their eyes punctured, and some lay with their pulpy entrails on the ground beside them.

Blade skirted the last intervening Vampire and reached Grizzly's side. He crouched and gripped the mutant's right shoulder. "Grizzly?"

The bear-man didn't stir.

"Grizzly?" Blade said, then rolled the mutant over carefully.

"Blade!" Sergeant Havoc shouted. "The Vampires!"

Blade looked up and glimpsed white figures moving in the rubble. So the Vampires hadn't left! They were preparing for one more charge.

A moan suddenly passed Grizzly's lips.

Blade bent down and shook the mutant's shoulder. "Grizzly? Can you hear me."

Grizzly's eyes flicked open. He focused on the giant and shook his head. "What the hell hit me?"

"I used explosives," Blade explained.

"The least you could do is warn a guy," Grizzly muttered, pushing himself up on his elbows. He surveyed the carnage and grinned. "Not bad. I haven't had this much fun in ages."

"Are you hurt? Can you stand?" Blade inquired.

"I'm fine," Grizzly insisted, rising.

Blade stood, shifting his attention to the ruins. "They're getting set to try again. We're better off on the rim." He headed upward.

Grizzly followed, his tread unsteady.

"Are you sure you can manage?" Blade questioned.

"I'm fine," Grizzly reiterated. "Just woozy. A few deep breaths and I'll be as good as new."

Blade stared to his right and spied the remains of Corpus. "You did a number on him," he remarked.

"The sucker had it coming!" Grizzly responded.

"I thought he was trying to talk you to death at first," Blade mentioned casually.

"He did love to flap his gums," Grizzly agreed.

"What were you two talking about?" Blade asked.

"Nothing much."

Blade, his broad back to the mutant, grinned.

Sergeant Havoc was on his knees when the pair climbed over the edge. "I'm glad to see you made it," he said to the mutant.

"Not half a glad as I am," Grizzly replied.

"There's a lot of activity down there," Havoc informed Blade. "They won't stop for anything this time."

"We have your backpack," Blade noted. "We'll give them another explosive surprise."

Grizzly glanced at the Warrior. "Anything I can do?"

"Leave."

"What?" Grizzly asked in surprise.

"Leave," Blade repeated. "Get out of here while you still can. We've held the Vampires long enough to insure they can't catch Athena, Boone, and Thunder. Now I want you to leave." He nodded at the battlefield. "I estimate there were over one hundred and twenty after us initially. I don't know how many we've killed. Half. Maybe more. But that still leaves a lot down there, and they'll be fired up, thirsty for our blood. Havoc is right. They won't stop this time. And for all we know, more could show up."

"So why aren't *you* leaving?" Grizzly demanded.

"I would if I could," Blade said. "There's no need to buy the others time. But I won't desert Havoc, and he can't run with his injured leg."

"Well, if you're not leaving, I'm not leaving," Grizzly declared. "And that's final."

"I don't want either of you to stay on my account," Sergeant Havoc interjected.

"I'm the head of this unit," Blade reminded the noncom. "I don't abandon my people."

Sergeant Havoc gazed over his left shoulder at the eastern horizon. "The sun's coming up. The Vampires will want to get this over with as quickly as they can."

"Then let's make sure they don't," Blade said, kneeling and putting a new magazine in the M-16.

"I guess I'll take a snooze," Grizzly quipped. "Wake me if you need me."

"We need you," Blade said. He picked up Sergeant Havoc's backpack and rummaged inside for one of the packets of explosive with a timer and detonator.

"You want me to lob that thing?" Grizzly deduced.

Blade removed a packet and hefted it. "When I give you the word, set the timer for one minute. Don't throw it until I say so."

"Just don't forget I've set the timer," Grizzly cracked.

Blade tossed the packet to the mutant, then shoved the backpack over. "Stay behind us. I don't want you hit."

"With a big lug like you in front of me," Grizzly said, "they won't even see me."

"That's what I'm counting on," Blade stated.

Sergeant Havoc lifted his M-16. "Here we go again."

The Venesects began their third concerted attack. Their features set in grim lines, their legs flying, they glided over the terrain in a compact mass, the point of their column going straight for their foes on the eastern rim. The crater wall partially shielded them from the light of the rising sun.

Havoc sighted on the column. "I want to thank the two of you for sticking with me," he commented.

"I've got nothing better to do," Grizzly said.

Blade took a bead on the front cluster of Vampires. "When they're at the base of the slope," he stated.

"Got you," Havoc acknowledged.

"I need to tinkle," Grizzly remarked.

A cry of collective rage erupted from the swarm of Venesects as they reached the foot of the incline.

"Now!" Blade bellowed.

The Warrior and the noncom leaned over the edge, firing indiscriminately.

This time the frenzied Vampires did not even slow down. As those first in line fell, those to the rear scrambled or vaulted over their comrades. Their earlier failures had served to arouse their wrath to a fever pitch. They were not accustomed to losing in combat, and being repulsed twice by a pair of humans and a mutant was more humiliation than they could bear.

Blade emptied his magazine and grabbed for another. He was smacking it home when he spotted the trio leading the upsurging horde: Polidori, Loring, and . . . Minshi! The enormous Vampire was still alive! He suppressed his amazement and glanced over his right shoulder at Grizzly. "The timer!"

Grizzly nodded and began turning the black dial.

Blade resumed firing, aiming at the three leaders. He sighted on Loring and squeezed the trigger, and was rewarded by the Vampire catapulting backwards onto the slope. Polidori was next. Blade shot him squarely in the face.

The Venesects were halfway to the rim.

"Throw it!" Blade bellowed.

Grizzly stepped to the edge and heaved the backpack with all of his strength.

All three Force members hit the dirt.

Footsteps were pounding close to the edge of the crater when the explosives detonated. Again the ground shook and bucked, only worse than before. A scorching blast of air engulfed Blade, Havoc, and Grizzly, to be replaced moments later by the dense, swelling dust cloud.

Coughing, with particles of red dirt in his nostrils and his lungs, Blade staggered erect, his ears ringing. He peered into the cloud, wondering if the explosion had stopped the Vampires, had sent them scurrying for the cover of the ruins.

It hadn't.

Murky forms materialized in the whirling red dust.

Vampires. With Minshi at their head.

Blade and the huge Venesect were less than a yard apart when they saw one another.

Minshi reacted instantly, lunging and grabbing the barrel of Blade's M-16, then twisting his body to the left as he pulled on the weapon.

Blade released the M-16. There was no time to waste in grappling for the rifle when more Vampires were coming over the rim. He whipped out his Bowies and took a step toward Minshi as the Vampire cast the rifle aside and backed up two strides.

What was this?

Why would the big Vampire back off?

Blade crouched, his Bowies extended, taking a wary step forward.

Minshi unexpectedly smiled, his right hand drifting behind his back, and when it reappeared a second later, his fingers were wrapped around the handle of a large carving knife.

The Warrior's gray eyes narrowed in bewilderment. The Vampire was offering him a fair fight! But why would—

Minshi suddenly swept the carving knife in a curving strike, then again as Blade evaded the keen edge. The Vampire tried to seize the upper hand with a wild series of swings and thrusts, ever the aggressor, constantly driving the Warrior backwards.

Blade caught sight of Grizzly and Sergeant Havoc to his right, side by side, taking on seven or eight Venesects. He saw Havoc slam the palm of his right hand into a Vampire's nose. The distraction proved costly. In the fraction of a second that the Warrior's eyes alighted on his friends, his adversary sprang forward and stabbed the carving knife up and in. Blade tried to jerk his upper body to the rear, but too late.

Minshi's carving knife sliced into the Warrior's left shoulder, penetrating the black leather vest and scraping his collarbone.

The Warrior dodged to the left, searing agony lancing his shoulder. He felt his blood spreading across his shoulder, upper back, and chest.

Minshi smirked and came on, the carving knife coated red.

Blade had to rely on his right arm, parrying four lightning stabs before he held his ground, refusing to retreat any farther. The Bowie and the carving knife produced muted clangs as the blades met again and again. Blade held his left arm at his side, conveying the impression it was useless. He wanted Minshi to step in closer or feint to his left.

Minshi feinted.

And Blade was ready, his grip slightly slippery because of his dripping blood. He held fast and plunged the left Bowie to the hilt in the Vampire's chest.

Minshi gasped and doubled over.

Blade had learned his lesson from their first fight. He'd stabbed the Vampire twice in the chest earlier, and yet Minshi had survived. So one more chest strike was nothing more than a minor inconvenience. Blade wanted to end their conflict permanently. His right Bowie flashed up, spearing into the Vampire's left eye, imbedding the upper third in the socket.

An almost comical expression of astonishment etched the Vampire's face. He voiced a strangled cry of baffled desperation and reached for the Warrior's right arm.

Blade tugged the Bowie free.

Tottering backwards, Minshi placed his left hand over his ravaged eye. He tottered all the way to the brink of the crater. The dust had settled sufficiently to reveal the baleful gleam in his right eye as he toppled over the edge and vanished.

The Warrior turned to the right.

Grizzly was holding his own, his claws hacking and ripping in fearless abandon.

Sergeant Havoc was on his left knee, valiantly resisting the pummeling of three Vampires.

Blade started toward the noncom when a pair of strong arms enclosed his ankles and he tumbled onto his stomach. Something heavy struck the back of his head and the world seemed to spin and tilt. He managed to look over his left shoulder to find a Vampire with an M-16 in its hands. *His* M-16!

The Vampire was holding the rifle by the barrel. He growled and raised it for another blow.

And a strange thing happened.

A horizontal pattern of pink holes blossomed across the Vampire's chest and he was propelled through the air for over five feet.

Still dazed, and now confused, Blade was glancing in the direction of his companions when he saw a charging line of five Venesects cut in half at the waist as they appeared on the rim. A new sound filled the air, a pronounced whump-whump-whump, from overhead. Blade looked upward, and not until that moment had he appreciated how beautiful a helicopter could be.

There were four of them, one hovering over the three Force members, the others swooping over the crater in strafing runs, their big .50-caliber machine guns thundering in rhythmic precision.

Blade rose, realizing every Vampire on the rim was dead, and moved to the edge of the crater.

It was a slaughter. The choppers were picking off the Venesects as they attempted to reach the shelter of the Heartland. Heaps of perforated bodies littered the slope and the area between the incline and the ruins. A few of the Vampires succeeded in reaching cover, but for every one who did, five didn't.

Someone was laughing.

Blade looked to his right and discovered Grizzly and Sergeant Havoc a few feet from him, the mutant supporting the noncom under the left arm.

Grizzly gave an elated whoop. "Look at those turkeys run! We did it! We won!"

"Hey, Blade!" someone called down from above.

The Warrior tilted his head back.

Boone, Thunder, and Athena were in the chopper overhead, in the open bay. The helicopter was hovering at an angle. They smiled and waved.

Blade waved once, then stared at the floor of the crater.

There wasn't a living Venesect in sight.

# CHAPTER TWENTY-THREE

The four helicopters were on the ground 50 yards from the east wall of the crater. Green tents had been pitched near the rim. Sentries were on duty on all sides to safeguard against a surprise counterattack. The afternoon sun was hot, and a warm wind stirred the red dust.

Blade and Bear emerged from a tent in the middle of the row and walked to the edge. The Warrior stared at the ruins, reflecting, and sighed.

"What's the matter with you, bro?" Bear asked.

"This was sloppy," Blade said.

Bear scrutinized the floor of the crater. The burial detail had spent the previous two days digging mass graves, and the majority of the Venesects were now decomposing under mounds of earth. "What are you talkin' about? We whipped their butts."

"But we didn't win."

"I think that knock upside your head rattled your brains," Bear commented with a grin.

"We defeated the Vampires," Blade said, "but we didn't win. How can we call any victory complete if some of the Vampires are still alive?"

A squad of Rangers marched into the daylight from the mouth of a passageway.

"Here comes Sergeant Montalbano," Bear observed. "Maybe he has some good news."

"I hope so," Blade said.

The squad passed the mass graves and ascended the incline. Segeant Montalbano, a wiry man with a clipped black mustache, saluted the Warrior.

"Report," Blade directed.

"The sweeps of the lower levels are continuing," Montalbano detailed. "Captain Ryan intends to spend another night down there to finish the mopping up."

Blade gazed at the solitary spire a half mile distant. Captain Ryan was a seasoned, competent officer, and the 190 Rangers in the Company were dedicated personnel. He recalled the relief he'd felt as the big helicopters had landed and disgorged their complements of about 50 men apiece. The Rangers had been spoiling for combat with the Vampires, but the Venesects were nowhere to be found.

"One more thing, sir," Sergeant Montalbano mentioned.

"Yes?"

"Captain Ryan found more humans," Montalbano divulged.

Blade looked at the trooper. "Alive?"

Sergeant Montalbano frowned. "No, sir. They were dead, like all the rest. Captain Ryan believes they were prisoners. They had those needle marks all over their bodies." He paused. "They were torn apart."

"The Vampires vented their wrath on the captives," Blade speculated.

Sergeant Montalbano reached into his right front pocket. "Captain Ryan asked me to give you this."

"What is it?"

Montalbano pulled a small brown wallet into view. "Captain Ryan told me to give this to you. He said it concerns the woman you mentioned. He said you'd understand."

Blade took the square of brown leather and flipped it open. A faded color photograph, tucked into a plastic strip, drew his attention. The picture showed a young boy and girl, both in their early teens or thereabouts, smiling broadly into the camera.

Their eyes conveyed their vitality and happiness, and they were hugging one another in sincere affection.

Bear leaned toward the Warrior for a glimpse of the photo. "Who are they?"

"The boy is Ethan Hogue," Blade answered softly. "The girl was his sister, Greta."

"Strange, the way she died," Sergeant Montalbano remarked.

"You saw her body?" Blade asked.

"Yes, sir," Montalbano responded. "In a room with four others. Their necks had been broken, their arms ripped from their bodies, and two were mutilated." He nodded at the photograph. "But not her. She wasn't mutilated. She died a clean death."

"How do you mean?"

"She was the only person we've found who was stabbed," Montalbano revealed. "All the others died horribly, but there she was, her arms folded in her lap, lying on the floor with a knife in her left eye."

Blade stiffened. "A what?"

"A knife," Sergeant Montalbano said. "A big carving knife. It was really strange."

Bear noticed a ripple of . . . something . . . register on the Warrior's face for a second. "What is it?"

Blade looked at the photograph, then at Montalbano. "Is there anything else?"

"No, sir," Montalbano said. "With your permission, I'd like to return to Captain Ryan."

"Go ahead," Blade ordered. "We don't need you topside."

Sergeant Montalbano started to turn.

"Sergeant?"

"Yes, sir?"

"Would you stop at the graves and find the sergeant in charge of the burial detail?"

Montalbano nodded. "Sergeant Harrell, sir?"

"That's his name," Blade said. "Would you ask him to report to me on the double?"

Sergeant Montalbano saluted. "Yes, sir." He wheeled and led his squad down the incline.

"What was that all about?" Bear inquired.

"Maybe nothing," Blade replied.

"Uh-huh," Bear said. In all the years he'd known the Warrior, he'd never seen this kind of reaction. It was weird.

Blade clasped his hands behind his back and surveyed the Heartland. "Where are the others?"

"Grizzly and the bunch?"

The Warrior nodded.

"In the mess tent, the last I saw," Bear said. "The medics have tended to Havoc. They say his leg will be as good as new in a couple of weeks." He chuckled. "They were real surprised."

"At what?"

"Those herbs Thunder used," Bear replied. "The herbs saved Havoc's life. Prevented the infection from spreadin' any worse than it did."

Blade watched as Sergeant Montalbano approached Sergeant Harrell.

"So tell me true," Bear stated bluntly. "What do you think of 'em?"

"Who?" Blade responded absently.

"Grizzly and the others," Bear said. "I volunteered to serve a year in your outfit. I'd like to know what I'm getting myself into."

"I'd stake my life on any one of them," Blade declared.

"That says a lot," Bear commented. "They're quite a crew. I think I'll get to like 'em."

"You will."

Sergeant Montalbano and Sergeant Harrell conversed briefly, and Sergeant Harrell jogged toward the east rim.

"Where do we go when we're done here?" Bear asked.

"To the Force facility north of LA," Blade answered.

"I'm lookin' forward to gettin' some time off later," Bear mentioned. "I hear they have some stone foxes in Los Angeles."

"The foxes are nice," Blade agreed, his voice subdued. "But I liked the elephants better."

Bear did a double take. "Say what?"

"Jenny and I took Gabe to the LA zoo," Blade explained. "We'd never seen a zoo before. Gabe had a great time."

Bear stepped over to the Warrior and nudged Blade's left elbow. "Hey. What's eatin' you?"

The Warrior glanced at his friend. "Nothing. Why?"

"You're a lousy liar," Bear noted. "And you haven't been payin' attention to a word I said."

"I did too," Blade insisted.

Sergeant Harrell came over the crest and walked up to Blade. He saluted. "You wanted to see me, sir?"

Blade stared at the mounds of dirt. "Yes, sergeant. Have all the Venesects been buried?"

"Almost, sir," Harrell answered. "We have a few left. And there's a pile of legs and arms and stuff. That's it."

"Good," Blade commented. "I don't want the rotting corpses to attract any more mutants."

"Yes, sir," Sergeant Harrell said. "We had a hell of a time with those three bugs the first night."

Blade pursed his lips.

"Was that all?" Sergeant Harrell questioned, appearing perplexed.

"Did you notice anything unusual about any of the Vampires you buried?" Blade inquired.

"Unusual, sir?" Sergeant Harrell repeated. "No. They all looked pretty much the same to me."

"Did you happen to see a Vampire larger than all the rest?" Blade asked. "One about my size?"

"No, sir," the Ranger replied.

"Would you check with your men? I'd like to know."

Sergeant Harrell shrugged. "I'll check, sir, but it might not do much good. We've been busting our butts, carrying all those bodies to the graves and throwing them in. After you do ten or twenty, you stop paying much attention."

"I understand," Blade said. "But check for me."

"Yes, sir." Harrell saluted and trotted off.

Blade unclasped his hands and looked at Bear. "They won't find his body."

"Whose body?"

"A Vampire by the name of Minshi," Blade stated.

"So what's the big deal over one Vampire?" Bear probed.

"It isn't every day that I kill someone and he doesn't die," Blade responded.

"What?"

"Nothing," Blade said, shaking his head. His eyes roamed over the Dead Zone to the east. "Too bad there aren't any trees around here?"

"Trees?"

"Yeah," Blade confirmed. "Maybe we should have used wooden stakes after all." He walked toward the tents.

Wooden stakes? Bear scratched his chin as he followed the Warrior. There was no doubt about it. His buddy was gettin' downright weird.

# EPILOGUE

She found him standing near the helicopters, his shoulders slumped, his arms at his sides, staring into space. "There you are! I've been looking all over for you."

Grizzly turned, his features softening at the sight of her. "Hi, Athena."

"Why'd you take off all by yourself?" Athena asked. "I missed you."

"You did?"

"Of course, dummy," she said.

Grizzly coughed lightly.

"I need your advice," Athena informed him. She gazed at the nearest chopper. "Those pilots sure can handle those babies, can't they?"

Grizzly nodded.

"What's with you?" Athena demanded. "Are you in one of your moods again?" She stretched, beaming contentedly. "We're alive! Do you realize how sweet life is? For a while back there, I was beginning to wonder if any of us would see daylight again."

"Is that why you're so cheerful?"

"That, and another reason," Athena told him. "Which is why I came looking for you."

"Oh?"

"Yep." She inhaled the air. "You and I are becoming quite close. Or didn't you notice?"

"I've noticed," Grizzly said quietly.

"Definitely," Athena stated. "I think you're the best friend I have."

Grizzly's eyes narrowed slightly. "Friend?"

"And as my friend, I expect you to be honest with me," Athena said.

"I'd never lie to you."

"I know." She glanced around to ensure they were alone. "So I need your advice."

"About what?"

Athena smiled. "One of the pilots has asked me out."

Grizzly's cheeks twitched. "Oh?" he commented nonchalantly.

"Yeah. And you know the reputation these fly-boys have," Athena noted.

"What kind?"

"A woman can't trust one as far as she can throw him," Athena said.

Grizzly cleared his throat. "So what advice do you need?"

"It should be obvious," Athena responded. "Do you think I should go out with him after we get back?"

The bear-man conducted a study of the knuckles of his right hand. "You're a big girl, Athena. You do what you want."

"What kind of advice is that?" Athena questioned. "I thought you'd be happy for me. You know I haven't been on a date in ages."

Grizzly raised his right hand and shielded his eyes from the sun. "I'm happy for you."

"Really?"

"Really."

"You don't sound happy."

Grizzly chuckled. "I guess I was hoping you'd want to go out with *me*."

Athena laughed and placed her hand on his shoulder. "I'll go out with you anytime. We're friends, remember?"

"I'll never forget it," he assured her.

"Aren't you glad fate threw us together?" Athena commented.

"If Fate was here in person," Grizzly remarked, "I'd gut the sucker."

She laughed again. "You're crazy! You know that?"

Grizzly nodded. "That's me. A wild and crazy guy."

Athena started toward the tents. "I'm going to tell the flyboy yes. Want to come along?"

"I wouldn't want to intrude on you two lovebirds."

"Lovebirds? We haven't even been on our first date yet!"

"You know how fast those pilots work," Grizzly observed wryly.

Athena paused. "You're not going to stay out here the rest of day, are you?"

"I thought I'd work on my suntan."

She giggled. "Be serious."

"I'm always serious."

Athena shook her head. "You *are* in one of your moods again. What brings these mood swings on?"

"Hormones."

She stared at him for a moment. "Don't stay out here too long. Please. As a favor for me."

"Your wish is my command," Grizzly said.

"See you soon," Athena stated, and blew him a kiss. She strolled away, whistling.

Behind her, Grizzly's shoulders moved in a peculiar up-and-down fashion.